When
Lightning
Strikes

Crossings of Promise

When Lightning Strikes

When Lightning Strikes

Hugh Alan Smith

Herald
Press

Waterloo, Ontario
Scottdale, Pennsylvania

National Library of Canada Cataloguing in Publication Data
Smith, Hugh Alan, 1954-
  When lightning strikes

(Crossings of promise)
Includes bibliographical references.
ISBN 0-8361-9164-1

  I. Title. II. Series

PS8587.M5383W46 2001   C813'.6   C2001-900927-5
PR9199.4.S64W46 2001

The paper used in this publication is recycled and meets the minimum require-
ments of American National Standard for Information Sciences—Permanence
of Paper for Printed Library Materials, ANSI Z39.48-1984.

English Scripture is from the New International Version. German Scripture
is from *Die Bibel*, translated by Martin Luther.

WHEN LIGHTNING STRIKES
Copyright © 2001 by Herald Press, Waterloo, Ont. N2L 6H7
  Published simultaneously in USA by Herald Press, Scottdale, Pa.
  15683. All rights reserved
Canadiana Entry Number: C2001-900927-5
Library of Congress Catalog Control Number: 2001088539
International Standard Book Number: 0-8361-9164-1
Printed in the United States of America
Cover art by Dolores Caldwell
Book and cover design by Gwen M. Stamm

10 09 08 07 06 05 04 03 02 01 10 9 8 7 6 5 4 3 2 1

To order or request information, please call 1-800-759-4447
(individuals); 1-800-245-7894 (trade).
Website: www.mph.org

To Mom, for gifting me with your love,
and the love of literature.
We'll meet in glory.

Paul's Journey in Europe

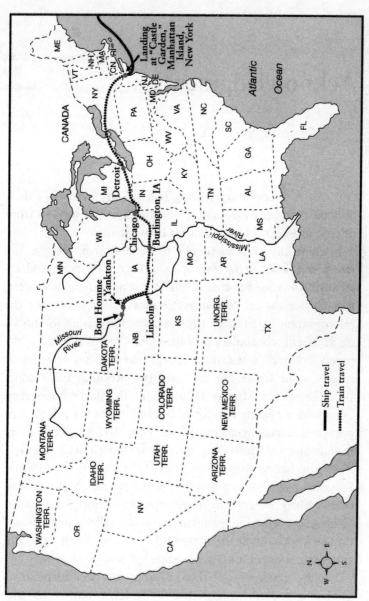

Paul's Journey in America

Acknowledgments

People say writing is a solitary activity. This is only partly true. Without at least some help and support from others, most books would never be written.

I extend my grateful thanks to the following people: my wonderful wife, Beth, for the love, encouragement, and insight (this is your book as much as it is mine); my daughters, Danica (for the creative storyline ideas) and Nicola (for the photographic assistance); my friends at the colony for advice on Hutterite vocabulary and lifestyle; Tony Waldner for the timely research assistance; George Paetkau for translation help; Connie Jensen for the insightful proofing and editing; Dave Berry and Murray Polushin for the library resources; Bev Holder, Leanne Baudistel, and others for the prayer support and encouragement. All of you, and so many more friends and associates, have helped me more than I can say.

I'd also like to thank David Garber and the staff at Herald Press for believing in this work. And a special thanks goes to editor Mary Meyer for so perceptively refining the manuscript and overseeing the metamorphosis called publication. I don't even know the many things you do, but from a stack of earthbound paper a book has emerged and taken wing.

Finally, thank you, T. Davis Bunn, for your inspiration, guidance, and selfless generosity. You have touched my life, almost as a hand divine.

Contents

Chapter 1

The Funeral

After the brightness outside, everything in the church was dark and shadowy. I forced myself to walk up the narrow corridor toward the terrible truth.

The right half of the church was a sea of black coats and beards. That was the men's side. On the left, like a field of sad-eyed flowers, were the women, their faces serious and pale in dark kerchiefs. Everyone was alike in clothing and expression.

We Hutterites were used to being the same. For over three hundred fifty years, we had worshiped together, lived together, died together. Always helping, always sharing, always the same.

But I knew nothing would ever be the same for me again. All I wanted to do was get away. I might have turned and run back into the sunshine, except for my *Basel* and *Vetter*—my aunt and uncle. Sannah, my mother's tight-lipped sister, and her husband, Andreas, were right behind me, forcing me on. On toward the awful sight of two smooth, pine-board coffins placed end-to-end in the aisle of the church.

Oh, how I wished I had never prayed to go to America.

I felt my aunt's thumb in my back, nudging me forward. I took my place on the bench reserved for family beside the open coffins. The village preacher stood up to lead the hymn singing. Two hundred voices filled the room with somber rhythm and sound. Sad yet peaceful, it filled the emptiness in my heart just a little bit.

I let my gaze wander, drifting through the room until it came to rest on the still figure in the coffin in front of me. My *Mueter*, my own dear mother. A curl of rolled hair curved out from under her kerchief. Her hair was the clean pale yellow of autumn grass in the sun, the autumn grass of the Russian steppes where we lived. I bit my lip, remembering how I had often buried my face in that hair as Mueter read the Bible or sewed and sang. Such long, thick, glorious hair.

Like all Hutterite women, my mother had never let her hair be cut. In public it was wrapped under her kerchief, but in the privacy of our home she would shake it loose so it flowed across her shoulders and down her back like a waterfall in a golden sunset. How I wanted to lose myself in that hair now, and feel the comfort of her embrace. But it would not happen again.

Nor would I ever again feel *Fater's*—my father's—guiding hand on my shoulder, or feel his strong, work-hardened hands lift me into the air as they had done so often in the past. There he lay, in the wooden box in front of my mother's. His hands, like Mueter's, were hidden under the funeral cloth instead of resting in the open. I knew why. I had seen what happened. Hands burnt black were too horrible for a public farewell.

Choking on the thick air, I looked away, toward the singing people around me, their mouths opening and closing like fish in the water. I was separated and alone on the uncrowded family bench by the caskets. At twelve years old, I had no brothers or sisters. This was strange, because Hutterite families were usually large. But something had gone wrong when I was born, and Mueter could have no more children. It had made my parents sad, but Mueter said it helped them love me all the more.

Now I had to live with this stern-faced aunt, my mother's sister, who was sitting across from me. Five of her children were grown and gone, so I would still be an only child. Her ability to love was gone too, since Cousin Daniel's death five years earlier. I was the same age Daniel had been when pneumonia took him, but I knew Sannah Basel would never find me good enough to replace her favorite child.

The singing stopped, and the preacher opened his book to begin the three-hundred-year-old funeral service. He talked for three-quarters of an hour. Then he closed the book, and two men put lids on the coffins. I took a last look as the lids came down. My mother's golden hair disappeared in the shadow, and I wanted to crawl in with her, let them put the lid over us both so I would not have to face the world. I knew it was impossible. I was alive. Mueter was dead, never again to walk in my world.

Relatives and friends, four for each coffin, lifted my parents' bodies and carried them out. We followed the wagon to the village edge for the burial.

When they went into the ground, first Mueter, then Fater, I should have cried. I wanted to. But I couldn't, not after what I had done. I could only think of my hateful prayer. I hadn't wanted it to turn out this way.

With an effort I lifted my gaze to the faces around the grave. All eyes were downcast, as serious and brooding as the cold place in the bottom of my heart. All, that is, except one pair of eyes—the most luminous, large brown eyes I had ever seen. They belonged to a girl about my age. I didn't recognize her, so I knew she was not from our village of Hutterdorf. Staring straight at me, those eyes seemed to reach inside, gently touching my pain. Suddenly it took all my strength to keep my tears locked inside. But, no, I did not deserve to cry.

I looked away as the preacher's final prayer floated off on the breeze to lose itself in the vastness of the empty sky.

Shovels flashed and dirt lumps thumped hollowly in the hole. And still I did not weep. I only wished that I had never prayed to go to America.

Chapter 2
The Grave

With the burial over, people began filing out of the little cemetery. Now I would be in Sannah Basel's hands. Though I knew she didn't like me, she was probably glad to be in charge so she could teach me a thing or two about right living.

She believed all Christians were supposed to live communally. Didn't the Bible say the disciples shared everything they had with one another so no one would be needy? That was why our ancestors had started the first colonies in Moravia back in the fifteen hundreds. But here in Russia, communal life had fallen apart. For forty years now, every family had been on its own.

But a few years ago, three preachers had gotten the communal life going again. That's where the problem lay with Sannah Basel. She and Andreas Vetter had joined the colony, but Mueter and Fater had not.

"Will you defy God?" Sannah Basel had shouted at my parents.

Fater had replied, "We can love Jesus as deeply from here as inside the colony."

"Then what about Preacher Michael Waldner's vision? Don't you know an angel asked him how many survived the great flood in Noah's time?"

"Yes, Sannah, and only those on the ark survived."

"So the angel said, 'Now you know your place. The ark is the *Gemeinschaft* of the Holy Spirit to which you no longer belong.' Will you not know *your* place, Zechariah?"

"Whatever Preacher Michael saw or did not see is his own affair," my father had answered, ending the discussion. "It is not for me."

Sannah and my parents had never got along after that. And now she had her chance to turn me into the kind of Hutterite she wanted. I would soon be on my way to live with them in their village of Sheromet.

I took one last look at the mound of dirt piled over the double grave. As I turned away, I wondered about the girl. The one with the big eyes. Why had she stared at me the way she did? It was as if she knew something about me, as if she were sticking her nose into my life. She didn't need to do, as far as I was concerned. I looked around to see if she was still watching, but all I could see was a mass of backs, bobbing and weaving away from me. The low, slanting rays of the late-day sun seemed to push the crowd out of the cemetery.

Sannah Basel was still talking to some people by the grave. I didn't want her dragging me off to Sheromet in the wagon right away, so I slipped out of the cemetery. I wanted to be alone, and I knew the place to go. No one would be grinding grain at the windmill today.

I went through the middle of Hutterdorf. The village was built in the Mennonite style, with all the houses lined up along a single street.

There, near the middle, was the house I had lived in all my life. The wrought iron rail along the top of the stone fence reminded me of the horror. I ran past it, all the way to the end of the village.

The big wooden windmill stood high like a giant tree stump. It could swivel in any direction to catch the wind, and its propellers shone in the sun like the silver wings of an enormous bird. Climbing the ramp to the main floor, I wished the windmill really did have wings that could fly me away from the village, back to a happier time.

Inside, the light was dim, but I knew my way around from watching the men grind grain. I climbed the smooth wooden ladder to the upper level where the shaft from the windmill propeller came in. A big gear on the end of it turned another shaft that went down to work the machinery below.

When the windmill was running, the hum and creak of the shafts and the grinding of the mill wheel made a strange music. The whole building vibrated like it was alive. Today, only the breeze stirred, whispering like a sad spirit through the propeller sails outside.

I sat down on a pile of old flour sacks and watched the dusty light streak in through one of the small windows. I couldn't help thinking about my parents, and my part in their death. I wished I had never heard of America.

Chapter 3

Lightning

In the past, armies and robber bands had persecuted Hutterites, killing men, doing terrible things to women, and burning colonies to the ground. To escape all that, our people had moved to Russia, where many Mennonites lived.

Hutterites were pacifists. We believed the Bible said we should not fight or be in armies. Normally, everyone in Russia had to take a turn in the army, but Russia was desperate for farmers, so Catherine the Great agreed that Hutterites and Mennonites could stay and farm, and skip the army. But now a new *Tsar*—Alexander II—had canceled the agreement.

Now all the Hutterites and Mennonites planned to leave. Our elders had sent men to see what America was like. They found out the Americans didn't need us in the army. There, it didn't matter what language you spoke or what religion you followed. Everyone was welcome, and there was lots of good land.

America! I could hardly wait to go.

Then one day Fater came in smiling, and said, "The Russian government has changed its mind."

Mueter and I looked at him blankly.

"They don't want to lose all their Mennonite and Hutterite farmers, so we will be allowed to take a turn at forestry service instead of the army."

"Is everyone staying?" Mueter had asked.

"Many Hutterites are going to America, anyway," he said, "but most Mennonites are staying."

"But Fater, we need to go!" I cried in alarm.

"No, Paul, farming is good here. Besides, there are still Indian wars in America."

• • •

I was alone in the house on the terrible day. Mueter and Fater were away at Sheromet to buy a stove from Sannah Basel and Andreas Vetter's colony, which was selling everything they could not take to America.

By evening I had a fire going in the living room's big brick stove. A storm was brewing outside, and the air was cool. Warm and comfortable by the fire, I dreamed about Indians and American gunfighters, even though guns were forbidden for Hutterites. The men who had been to America said the newspapers were full of stories about gunfighters like John Wesley Hardin, Jesse James, and the Younger brothers riding around shooting up the West like they weren't afraid of anything. Who could help being interested in that?

So I prayed about America. "Please God," I said, "make something happen so I can go there too."

I heard a rumble, and went to the window to look out. The sky was darkening. Night was coming, and storm clouds were piling up into high black towers. Lightning flashed in the distance, and another rumble rolled across the steppe. I wondered whether Mueter and Fater were out there on the road somewhere. They should have been home by now.

As I watched, the clouds grew bigger and darker. Rain spit, and lightning danced. Each flash split the darkness with blinding brightness. The apple trees in the orchard stood like scarecrows in the pulsing light. The buildings across the street glared like ghost houses. The wrought iron weather vane, my father's pride, flashed like a sword in the windy sky.

Wrought iron. It was fancy, and Fater liked to work it on the metal forge in the farm shed behind the house. Communal Hutterites did not go in for fancy metalwork. They said it was too worldly. But Fater said a little beauty was not a bad thing. Our stone fence was the only one in the village topped with a fancy row of twisted wrought iron, all the way to the gate. And it was the wrought iron that caused the grief.

The clouds were billowing and boiling now, and crashes of thunder came at almost the same instant as the lightning. I was getting worried. I remembered hearing how lightning had struck the Jake Kleinsasser house, burning it to the ground. The barn, which was joined to the house, had caught fire too. The pigs were trapped inside, and they had squealed like shrieking demons as they burned to death. What would I do if lightning started our house on fire?

Then, in another flash, I saw a wagon in the rain, just outside our gate. A man stood beside it, helping a woman down. Mueter and Fater were home! They glistened with rain. I must have heaved a great sigh of relief because the window fogged up from my breath. I wiped the glass quickly so I could see them come in. I smiled to think how grateful they would be for the warm fire I had burning in the stove.

And then it happened, the blazing scene that seared my brain forever. A crash shook the house like a cannon. At the same moment, fire ripped into the yard, shredding the air by the weather vane. Everything jumped into view, blasted to stillness in one frozen moment, an electrified flash of fire and light that I could never erase from my memory.

I saw Mueter and Fater, halfway through the gate, their bodies outlined in ripples of blue fire. Mueter was first, with Fater behind, his big hand holding the gate for her, and her smaller, delicate hand reaching back and touching the metal beside his. That was what killed them. The metal. From the weather vane, the blast of electricity ripped through the wrought iron rail, right to the gate they were holding, and burned their image forever into my eyes.

Mueter was looking back to Fater. His face was turned toward her. It should have been a perfect picture, a gentleman and his lady. But everything was ablaze with an unworldly power shot from the heavens, crackling and sizzling through their bodies, holding them in a terrible electrified grip.

It lasted only a second, but seemed like forever. And then the scene cooled to gray and began to move in slow motion. I saw it in jerky spasms of light from a dozen other flashing daggers in the sky. My mother's mouth was open in a cry I could not hear. I saw her body buckle and spin sideways through the gate. Then my father toppled behind her. In his black Hutterite clothes he was like a giant burnt tree, an arm extended like a branch, a hand slipping from the gate, blackened to the color of his sleeve. I saw him fall crazily to the ground inside the yard, landing beside my mother. The gate swung shut behind them.

Then it was over. The next flash revealed the two of them lying side by side, a curl of smoke hanging in the air above. I could not move. I could not think. I stared into darkness, unable to believe what I had seen. It could not be true! Maybe it was only a trick of the light and darkness.

But it was no trick. If it were, I would not have been there in the windmill after the funeral, tormented by the horrible memory. I opened my eyes to make it go away, but in the darkness of the windmill it made no difference. I could not escape the vision of my parents lying by the fence with the closed gate behind them.

I tried to imagine them as they had been before, talking and laughing at the dinner table. I tried to see Fater hitching horses to the plow, or Mueter wrapping her braided hair up under her kerchief. But the memory would not come. Only the rain and lightning, and their still bodies on the ground. And the gate—swinging shut behind them. And dirt lumps falling on the coffins in the darkness of the grave.

Suddenly, I knew in my heart the meaning of the gate. Mueter and Fater were gone. Forever. They had passed through the gate to eternity, and I would never see them again. A suffocating wave of loneliness came over me, as deep as the ocean to America. I buried my face in the pile of flour sacks, and sobbed.

After a time I heard footsteps on the floor below. They were careful steps, feeling their way through the shadows. Then the ladder to my hideaway creaked. Who was it? I held my breath.

A voice rose through the trap door. "Paul. Come Paul, I have been looking for you everywhere. Why are you hiding at such a late hour?"

It was Andreas Vetter, my uncle. We should have been on our way to Sheromet, and he was bound to be angry. I heard him climb through the trapdoor. "Answer, Paul. Is it you?"

"*Joh,* Vetter—yes, Uncle," I said, and I could feel the heat of his exertion as he hauled himself up beside me.

Chapter 4

Sannah's Anger

Andreas Vetter's hand bumped my leg as he reached to find me in the dark. Then it was on my shoulder. I thought he would punish me for sure. But, puffing from his climb up the ladder, he said only, "I have been looking for you. I was going to get the whole village searching, but a man told me you like the windmill. So I came."

He waited, but I said nothing.

Finally he sighed. "A windmill is a good place to think. It is like life, is it not?"

What was he talking about? Wasn't a windmill just a machine? And why wasn't he angry?

Andreas Vetter went on. "You see, Paul, a windmill has one purpose—to keep its vanes in the wind and do the work it was made for. Lazy winds, playful winds, hard steady winds—the windmill faces them all.

"That is how we are, Paul. No matter what life brings, we must face it squarely and do what we are meant to do."

I wondered if he was crazy, rambling like that.

"But there is an exception, as you know. When the *buran* comes, smashing everything in its fury, the windmill must fold its arms out of harm's way to avoid being blown to pieces."

Andreas was talking about the fearsome steppe buran, the terrible storm that sometimes swept across the Russian steppe-land where we lived.

"Paul, you are right to have curled yourself up in your grief for a while, to hide from the world. You have suffered too much. But what happens to the windmill when the buran is over?".

Grudgingly, I answered, "The miller starts it again."

"*Joh*, Paul, the miller starts it." Andreas Vetter patted me on the shoulder. "It is time for you to face life again. But not alone. Jesus is your miller. Ask God to help you get on with the purpose he has for you."

So that was it. "God has no purpose for me," I said darkly. "Not any more."

Andreas' hand tightened on my shoulder. "Paul, God's purpose for you is to serve him and trust him. Start with that, and the rest will come."

It sounded good, but I had no idea how to serve God. And how could I trust a God who answered prayers the way he had answered mine? I had no reply for my uncle. So we sat, unhearing, unseeing. There was only the touch of his hand on my shoulder to tell me he was there.

"But come," he said finally. "We must join Sannah. She is waiting to get on the road."

• • •

Sannah Basel was grim on the way to Sheromet. Because of me, we had to drive the eight and a half miles south from Hutterdorf in the dark. Nothing but the hollow clip of the horses' hooves and the jingle of harness broke the stiff silence.

When we got to Sannah and Andreas' home I carried my suitcase into the house. I was so tired I could have fallen asleep on the wooden floor. I wanted only a bed. That was when Sannah started in. Her voice was high and piercing, like sharp sticks jabbing at my weary mind.

"Now Paul," she said, "I'm disappointed in your behavior today. Sorrow is no excuse for undisciplined behavior. You are in our family now, and I will not have you nursing your grief."

I scowled and stared at her defiantly. *Old flabber-mouth.*

Then she got louder. I was afraid she would wake the neighbors, especially since these houses in Sheromet were not real houses. They were long buildings, in the old Hutterite style, with eight apartments in each. In Hutterdorf, my home village, every family had its own house and yard. Here, others lived just behind the walls.

"You will not be surly in my house, and I will not tolerate disrespect. The Lord knows you have had a bad time, but you will behave and obey." She paused to catch her breath. "Now you will rest for a new day tomorrow. Your uncle will take you upstairs to your room."

When I turned to go, she added, "He will discipline you for running off and hiding today."

Up to now, Andreas Vetter had said nothing, but he finally tried to speak. "You know, dear, do you think this is the best way to start out? I—"

"There will be no spoiling him, Andreas. He needs to learn right from wrong, and he had best start learning now."

To hear Sannah Basel, you would think my parents had taught me nothing. *But of course they didn't live communally,* I thought bitterly. At least Andreas Vetter had some sense, but he wouldn't stand up to her. He took my arm and led me up the stairs. I was about to get my first lesson from Andreas Vetter's leather strap.

Chapter 5

Andreas' Strap

When we got upstairs Andreas Vetter was carrying the strap. Fortunately, like my father's, it was made from thin leather folded in half. Folded leather made a loud *pop*, but hurt less than a single thick strap.

Andreas made me bend over. I heard a whack as the leather bit my backside, then another whack. But it didn't hurt—he had missed. Then another whack, and it stung. And another, and he missed again. *He must be out of practice*, I thought. Then I realized Andreas was whacking the brown leather hassock beside me. One for me, one for the hassock, another for me, and another for the hassock. Then he left me out of it altogether, and the hassock got ten more.

If I hadn't felt so miserable, I would have laughed. It was the second time Andreas Vetter had gone easy on me when I expected worse. Maybe he wasn't so bad, though I wondered why he couldn't just tell Sannah I didn't deserve a licking. A Hutterite man was supposed to be in charge of the household. Just my luck to be stuck in a messed-up family.

Still, it was satisfying to think of Sannah downstairs thinking she heard the strap on my backside. She must have been disappointed not to hear me howl.

When he finished, Andreas Vetter straightened up and said wearily, "Now, you felt the ones on your hinder did you not, Paul? No one can say you did not get a licking.

"We shall leave for America in about three weeks," he added. "Until then, this shall be your room." Then he knelt with me, as my father had always done, and we said the nighttime prayer together. It was the same prayer used by all Hutterite families, communal-living or not.

> O almighty, eternal, and merciful God, you who have created all things in heaven, on earth, and in the sea, and who have made everything holy and good and through your grace have made us in your image—we thank you for it all. . . .

It was a long prayer—more than 400 words. I once counted them on a paper of my father's. Tonight the worst part was the prayer for parents.

> O holy Father, we who are still very young pray to you with all our hearts for our parents, whom you have given us through your grace and set in authority over us. Give them grace and strength, understanding and wisdom, to bring us up according to your divine will, to keep us from evil and to teach us what is good.

I could hardly speak, and even Andreas Vetter's voice sounded rusty. How could my parents teach me to be good from the bottom of a grave? If God had given them to me according to his will, why did he take them away again? I shuddered when I thought of the reason.

When the prayer was finished, Andreas Vetter was quiet. Then he said, "Paul, you must think of me and Sannah Basel as your parents now. We are here to take care of you."

Then he turned toward the door. "Try to mind your aunt. It will go easier for everyone. Good night, Paul."

What a strange introduction to my unwanted home. I was worn out. It seemed like weeks since my dear parents' funeral, though it had been just that afternoon. And there was tomorrow to face. I lay in bed, glad that it was dark. Quietly, I cried myself to sleep.

• • •

In a blink, the morning sun was shining through the little window in my room. I felt the warmth where it played on my face. I crawled out of bed. My Sunday clothes—black pants and jacket and white shirt—were gone. I pulled on my everyday black pants and long blue shirt, and put a belt around my waist. Then I lifted my chin to meet what the day would bring.

Something was missing, but at first I couldn't place it. My stomach growled, and I realized how hungry I was, having missed the funeral meal. Then suddenly I knew what it was. No cooking smells.

In my own home, the morning smell of bacon and eggs or oatmeal had always wafted from the stove. There would be the happy clink of pans and dishes as Mueter bustled in the kitchen. In this house there were no smells or sounds of cooking. In fact, there wasn't even a kitchen. Breakfast was prepared in the communal kitchen and dining hall, a separate building where everyone in the colony went to eat.

Sannah hustled me outside, then went to the kitchen. Since I was under fifteen, I had to wait until the adults finished eating before I could go in. I glanced around the colony village. Instead of being built on one long street, it was more of a square. In the middle were the church, the kitchen, and the kindergarten, with the long apartment houses around them. Only the timber and clay walls looked the same as at Hutterdorf.

It wasn't a long wait for breakfast. Only ten minutes after marching in, the adults were out. Immediately, children scurried from the apartments, like mice from a burning haystack, and trooped into the dining hall. I followed. A gray-bearded man asked me how old I was, and told me to sit between two boys about my size. We were lined up by age. The tables were in one row, as long as the room. The girls were at the far end, away from us boys.

Here it did smell good. As we sat down, an older woman and a couple of younger ones rushed out from the cooking area, plopping eggs and bacon on our plates. Nobody talked.

When the women left, the gray-bearded man looked down to the girls' end of the table and said, "Hannah."

The children bowed their heads. A strong, clear voice blessed the meal. Afterward, I looked over just in time to meet a pair of enormous brown eyes. It was the girl who had watched me at the funeral! I gaped in surprise.

The redheaded boy on my right jabbed me in the ribs. "What are you staring at?" he whispered. "You never hear a blessing, out there in the world?"

"I saw that girl yesterday, at the—I saw her in Hutterdorf," I replied, ignoring his obnoxious tone.

"It's Hannah Stahl," a smaller boy on my left said. "She's a strange one."

"Juseph!" the graybeard barked, hushing the talk. "Breakfast is for eating, not talking over." No one argued, but went back to wolfing their food. Five minutes later, we folded our hands as Juseph was chosen for the after-meal grace. Then everyone jumped up and filed out the door.

Chapter 6

Fight!

Sannah Basel had told me to join the gardener and the others after breakfast. Everyone scattered when we went outside, and I didn't see anyone who looked like a gardener. I did not want to go back to Sannah's, so I wandered around until a haystack by the colony barns caught my eye. I hopped a wooden rail fence to get to it.

A mound of hay lay along one side, where someone had been loading a wagon for feeding cows. Flopping onto it, I enjoyed the musty-sweet smell and pillow-like softness. I looked straight up at the sky. It was deep blue, with billowy clouds scattered across it like frothy milk tossed from a bucket.

One thing I had noticed about clouds was that they would always come out like faces if you let them. I used to wonder if God was in the clouds looking down at the world. Sure enough, I saw a face today, a big white-bearded frown in the sky. It was gruff and sneering, like a bad-tempered old man. *You got what you wanted*, it seemed to say. *Are you not happy now for your selfishness? Do you not think you deserve to be alone?* I shut my eyes and put my fingers in my ears. I would not listen. But the voice was not from the clouds. It was in my own head. I let my hands fall uselessly to the scratchy hay.

"Hey you, *faul Kind*, lazy boy! Will you lie around when there is work to be done?"

This voice was real. I opened my eyes. A man stood over me, blocking the sun. Unlike the face in the clouds, this one's beard was black. Always beards. With Hutterites every married man must have a beard. It was one of the rules.

"Oh, it is you—the new boy. Did no one tell you? You are supposed to be in the garden."

"I don't know where it is," I said.

"Well, I can tell you it is not in this haystack," he replied, not unkindly. Then he pointed to the western edge of the colony. "It is behind the hedge, over there."

The garden was enormous. It had to be, to feed more than a hundred people. Through the hedge I could see all the boys bobbing up and down, picking head lettuce. They crawled along the rows, working together like a machine. I was looking for a place to join when the redheaded boy from breakfast looked up and sneered at me. "So you finally decided to help a little, did you? Did you never work where you came from?"

Anger stirred in my gut.

"Lucky for you your ungodly parents died," he sneered, "or you would never have joined us on God's ark."

"Shut up!" I blurted out, my hands balled into fists. He should not have mentioned my parents.

He stood up and stuck his chin in my face. It was as high as my eyes. The muscles in his neck were bulging and tense.

"I don't shut up for any godless *Ausländischer*—not for any outsider." He shoved my chest with the heels of his hands, knocking me back a step.

My anger exploded. Lunging forward, I punched him in the gut with all my strength. Air whooshed out of his lungs, and as he doubled over I rammed my head forward and butted his nose. My cap flew off. Blood spurted from his face, into my hair and down my own face like a river.

He grabbed me and hung on. I didn't know if he was trying to wrestle me down or just stop me, but he called me some ungodly names. I wrapped my arms around him and shoved. We fell on top of the lettuce. I felt a head scrunch under his back, and my hand was slippery with juice. I wished it were his head, instead of just lettuce. I was so angry I wanted to kill the boy. I kicked and punched like a madman, and he screamed bloody murder.

Then a pair of big hands gripped my shoulders, and I was lifted into the air. The red-haired boy and I were still hanging on to each other, so he rose with me. Then the boy let go and fell back with a thud. I heard the air whoosh out of him again.

The big hands flipped me upright, and I found myself looking into a familiar stern face. It was the graybeard from the kitchen, the one who had watched over us at breakfast. *So you are the gardener*, I thought.

I must have been stupid with anger because I smiled right into his face. He was so surprised he dropped me on the ground like a scorching hot biscuit. The anger drained out of me, and for a second it all seemed so funny I thought I would laugh. But the next thing I knew, I was crying. I had won the fight, shocked the graybeard, and now I was standing in front of everyone, crying. I didn't even know why. It was embarrassing. But my strength had drained away with the anger, and I couldn't fight it.

All eyes were on me. I was alone in a garden of strangers, stupid tears running down my cheeks.

The gardener slapped his hands on his thighs and shouted to the other children to get back to work. I heard them shuffle away. In the gardener's hand was a handkerchief, which he used to cover the redhead's nose.

Graybeard waved me away. "Go home to wash yourself. I will call for you later."

Retreating through the hedge, I heard the slap of leather. The gardener was warming the boy's hinder with his belt.

Sannah Basel's was the last place I wanted to go. I slipped off to the edge of the colony, crossed a footbridge over a little creek by the duck pond, and entered a stand of trees.

It was quiet there, and I felt a bit of peacefulness slip through the sun-dappled leaves into my heart. Being alone by myself was better than being alone surrounded by people. Red-hair was right. I was an Ausländischer. And that was fine by me. I didn't want to be one of them. I was thankful for the trees that hid me.

But my solitude was short-lived. I had been there only a few minutes, sitting with my back against a tree, when the grass rustled behind me. Footsteps. Determined not to look, I stared straight ahead and braced myself for more trouble. The rustling stopped beside me. At any moment, a voice would order me home or to some workplace or to who knew where. But there was no sound. Only a quiet waiting.

Finally, curiosity got the better of me. Wondering whose beard I would stare up into this time, I turned my head. There was no beard. Just those big, brown eyes I had seen at the funeral.

Chapter 7

Hannah

"You!" I was surprised. "What do you want?" I asked gruffly.

"I saw you walk away, and decided to say hello."

"So, hello."

"You're not very friendly, are you?"

"Is there a reason I should be friendly?"

"Never mind," she said. Then there was silence. I could hear the breeze whispering through the leaves. It fluttered her dark skirt and gingham apron.

"They say your name is Paul," she said finally, trying to make conversation.

"They say right."

She tried again. "My name is . . ."

"Hannah," I interrupted.

She looked at me curiously. "How do you know?"

"The gardener, in the kitchen—he called you Hannah."

"You don't miss much do you?" Hannah replied, smiling.

"What's to miss?" I mumbled, wishing she would go away.

"Maybe you have something to miss," she said, suddenly serious. "I just wanted to tell you . . . well, to tell you I'm sorry."

Now I really wished she'd go away. But she kept looking at me with those big eyes that seemed to see right into me. I didn't want her to stir up any more tears. I'd had enough of crying.

"Why should you be sorry? It's not your fault."

"You know I didn't mean that," she replied, still staring.

"What are you looking at?" I grumbled.

Hannah smiled again. "Right now I am looking at blood, and dirt, and messed up clothes. Are you badly cut?"

"It's not *my* blood."

She leaned forward, looking for cuts. "Then whose?"

"The red-haired kid." She certainly was a nosy one.

"Hons Gross? He's the toughest boy on the colony!" She sounded impressed, and I couldn't help feeling a little smug.

"He lost to you?" she asked.

"He's the one who did the bleeding, isn't he?"

"Hutterites are not supposed to fight," she said matter-of-factly.

Now she was sticking me with guilt. "Don't you think I know that?" I growled angrily. "I am Hutterite too. Just because I don't live on a colony, do you think I know nothing about our religion? Anyway, if nobody around here fights, how do you know Red Hair is the toughest?"

"I didn't say nobody fights. I said we are not *supposed* to fight. Nobody's perfect, you know. Not even here. And if you weren't so busy trying to fight with me right now, you would know I'm only trying to be friendly."

"If you weren't so busy trying to be friendly, you would know I am trying to mind my own business," I snapped. But I knew I was being unfair. She didn't deserve my bad temper. "Okay. I'm sorry. I'm just a little grumpy right now. . . ."

She looked into me again with those compassionate brown eyes. They were so mysteriously sympathetic, I half wished I could tell her my terrible secret. But that could never be. There could be no sympathy for me.

"You should go home and clean up. You look like you've been in a war. And you know we Hutterites are against war." She was grinning when she said it. "That's why we're going to America, after all."

"I can't go there."

Hannah's eyes got even bigger. "Can't go to America?"

I had to smile. "No—to Sannah Basel's. There will be war for sure if she sees me like this."

"Don't you know?" Hannah asked. "This is her week to help with cooking. She will be at the kitchen, not the house."

"Oh." I was surprised. I was used to a mother who cooked at home. "She didn't tell me. Is everything done by schedules around here?"

"Mostly."

"I don't see how you put up with it all."

"It keeps the colony running smoothly. Anyway, I need to go. There's laundry waiting to be washed, and I'm supposed to be working."

And with that, she walked away. *What a strange one*, I thought. I decided to go wash.

I re-crossed the creek and walked stealthily along the stone wall of the building where Sannah lived. I glanced at a window as I passed, and almost jumped out of my skin. A monstrous face was staring right at me! I backed away in terror, then almost laughed at my foolishness. It was only my own reflection! But what a sight. One side of my face was red with dried blood. The other was smudged dirt-black, with streaks washed through from my eyes. Tears. Stupid tears. And the girl had seen the streaks. I had to get washed quickly.

When I opened the door to the house, I met a worse-looking face than my own. It was blotchy red with anger. Sannah Basel! What was she doing here?

"Fighting with the first boy you see!" she spat. "For shame." She stared at me, her arms folded and lips pursed in grim disapproval. I had nothing to say, so I stared back. It was a silent fight, with our eyes. I knew she wanted me to look away and make excuses so she would have more reason to wag her tongue at me. Well, I would not give her the satisfaction.

I wondered why she was not in the kitchen doing her cooking. Had Hannah tricked me to get me in trouble? But why would she? Probably Sannah had gotten out of work so she could jump on me when I showed up.

Finally Sannah's shoulders sagged and she unfolded her arms. "Did they teach you no discipline out there in the world?" she sighed. She pointed to a bucket by the woodstove in the middle of the room. "Go to the kitchen and get hot water. You will have to bathe." I walked toward the bucket.

"Never mind," she said suddenly, bustling past me. "I will get it myself. I do not want the whole colony seeing your disgrace. Go to the shed outside. There is a tub on the wall. Get it down and wait."

I did as Sannah Basel told me, and before long I was sitting in water just a little red from the washed-off blood, and a little gray from the washed-off dirt. If only I could wash away everything that had happened in the past week. If only I could wash away my selfish prayer, and come out of that bath feeling clean inside.

I did not go back to the garden that day, but worked for Andreas Vetter in the tannery. He was the tanner for the colony, making different kinds of leather out of cowhides, and sometimes a horsehide or two. Normally Andreas Vetter would have had hides soaking in different vats of brine, cleaners, and tanning solutions. Now the whole colony was getting ready to leave for America, so the tannery was shut down. Andreas Vetter was busy making leather bags and trunks for the move. The tannery was a dusky, mysterious place. I liked the smell—salty and biting and leathery-smooth, all at the same time.

There was a small rope-making machine at the tannery

Because we needed ropes for the move, I spent the afternoon feeding hemp into the machine and cranking a handle. It worked like magic, spinning three strands into a single fat rope. I liked the job, except for the men who came and went, asking me all the time how I liked being a member of the *Gemein*—the colony. I told one lie after another, saying it was fine. This communal life had too many people buzzing around.

The day might have ended all right, except that after supper Sannah told me I was to go see Johann Kleinsasser, the teacher, over at the schoolhouse. He taught the German Bible lessons as well as lessons in reading and writing.

School was in the same building as the church, though school was out now for the summer. Even the Bible lessons were interrupted because of the coming move. Walking through the doors of the big empty room, I saw a lamp glowing on the desk at the front. It cast only a small circle of light, making the room look like a cave. The teacher sat at the desk reading from a big, black Bible. He lifted his head as I approached, and my heart jumped into my throat. Graybeard! What was he doing here?

"You're not . . . I was supposed to see the teacher," I said.

"*Joh,* I called for you," he answered.

"I thought you were the gardener."

"Of course, the gardener and the teacher. It is all one job in the Gemein. It is also my job to punish the colony's wayward youngsters. But I did not summon you to discuss my duties. I must perform one instead.

"I do not know how it was in your village, but we must have discipline and order here, where we all live together. Fighting we cannot abide." From a drawer he pulled a strap—a firm, single-thickness belt of leather. My own Andreas Vetter had probably made it. "I believe both of you boys were at fault, and I have already dealt with Hons. Come and bend over."

Was a strapping to end every day in this place for me? I stepped forward with defiance in my heart. I had cried in front of this man once already. I would not do it again. I promised myself I would never cry again, so long as I lived in the Gemein. Graybeard raised his arm, and the strap whistled through the air.

Chapter 8

Graybeard's Strap

Graybeard knew how to use the strap. Andreas Vetter's slaps were like the brush of fly wings compared to these. And with the teacher, there was no hassock-whacking. Hot needles of pain pierced my backside like angry bee stings, until I wanted to scream. But I made no sound for Graybeard's pleasure. By the time he had finished, I tasted blood on my tongue from biting back my cries. I added one more person to the hate list in my heart.

One thing surprised me, though. When I turned to leave, he called me back. I stared straight into his face to rob him of the satisfaction of knowing he had hurt me. But I saw no pleasure in his eyes. They looked heavy and tired, like my father's the time a wagon rolled over *Pfeffer*, our dear little Pepper dog. The wheel had broken his back, and it broke Fater's heart to have to kill the dog.

"Paul," the teacher said, patting the Bible, "you know this book warns against sparing the rod. You must learn how to behave while you are young." He pointed to a verse and read:

Wie man einen Knaben gewöhnt,
So lässt er nicht davon, wenn er alt wird.

Train a child in the way he should go,
and when he is old he will not turn from it.

"This was for your own benefit, Paul. You should know that."

I did not bother to thank him.

"The rest is up to you," he continued. "You must decide against bitterness, and let God make your life into something good."

Something good? I wanted to shout. *Like my parents getting killed?* He would probably have said that was for my own benefit too. I would rather live without so many benefits.

• • •

One thing good about my fight with Hons Gross was the respect I got from the other boys, which was ironic, because I wasn't usually much for fighting. Hons gave me no more trouble. Some of the others even tried to get friendly, but I kept my distance. Eventually, only Hannah Stahl sought me out, always appearing out of nowhere.

During the next three weeks I adjusted to the routine of communal life as the colony members adjusted to the idea of leaving their community behind. America was another irony for me. Before, I had wanted to go. Now I would have traded everything to stay. How could I be happy, knowing that the price for my ticket to America had been the lives of my parents?

The Gemein land, buildings, and anything else that could not be taken on the journey, was sold. Unfortunately, so many people were going, there were not enough buyers for everything. Prices were at rock bottom. A wealthy Mennonite named Peter Epp bought all of Sheromet. It was a big purchase, and he got himself a bargain.

From my old town of Hutterdorf, the communal Hutterites and the non-communal ones who had been my parents' friends were also leaving. In fact, Fater had been buying some of them out. Now others would have to buy that land, and my father's land too. Because I was with Sannah and Andreas now, all the money we got from selling what we owned went to the Gemein.

Sannah Basel told me how lucky I was to be taken in by the colony. "Every person is looked after completely, all the way from the cradle to the grave," she said proudly. "The colony provides for all your needs."

Still, I could not help thinking that the colony got a good deal when they took me. Not every twelve-year-old comes with the proceeds from selling a house and a farm.

The day before we left, Andreas Vetter and some other men collected my parents' personal belongings. I could not go with them, because I had to help herd the cows to their new owner's farm. The men brought our things to Sheromet to be sold, and that very day a Mennonite from Molotschna came and took it all away.

Of Fater's things, I kept only a pocketknife. Its shiny, three-inch blade folded neatly into a white bone handle, grooved with dark brown cross-hatching for a grip. It was smooth from years of use, but the hinged blade was tight and sharp.

Of my mother's possessions, I wanted only one thing—a wooden cigar box. She had told me it came from a Russian government man who had visited the village years ago while investigating the Hutterite religion. She and Fater had invited him to dinner. He was always smoking, and he had left the box. Mueter kept it, for storing the few things she treasured most.

But the box was not among the items the men collected.

Andreas Vetter assured me he had not seen it.

"But it *must* be there," I insisted. "Please take me to Hutterdorf to look."

"We got everything," he replied. "The house is bare. If the box were there, we would have found it."

"It can't have disappeared," I insisted. "Unless someone stole it."

"No one would steal an old wooden box. Do not speak so rashly." It was Sannah Basel talking.

"Then it has to be somewhere in the house. Just take me to look!"

"There is no time. We still have much to do, and we travel first thing tomorrow. You must put worldly things behind you, Paul. They only perish with time, and will do your eternal soul no good. Set your heart on spiritual matters that stay with you forever."

Sannah Basel was not listening to me. My eyes burned at her unfairness, but I remembered my vow not to cry. I tried to argue. "But Sannah Basel, it is only one box. Just a small box. I want to have it."

"Enough! I have told you, there is no time." She whirled around and strode off, so I couldn't argue.

Andreas Vetter put his hand on my shoulder. "I would take you Paul, but your Basel is right. We have run out of time. And as I said, we emptied the entire house."

I turned and walked outside. One small box. Was that so much to ask? It could not be gone. I knew what I would do. It was, after all, only three in the afternoon.

Chapter 9

On the Road

Dust rose around my feet, powdering my shoes and pant legs. I had crept away from the colony, and now walked briskly down the narrow road. With eight and a half miles between Sheromet and Hutterdorf, I knew I would be late getting back. It was sure to cause trouble, but at least I would probably not be missed until suppertime. Boys were running about doing last-minute jobs for different bosses all over the colony. Anyone looking for me would think I was helping someone else.

The carry bag on my shoulder bumped uncomfortably with every step. It contained candles and matches wrapped up in a handkerchief, in case the shutters were closed and it was dark in the house. The rye bread and cheese, and the jar of water I had packed would make the walk more bearable. I only hoped I wouldn't meet anyone who might wonder what I was doing.

"Paul!" My heart leaped at the sound of my name, and I almost ran. *Am I caught already?* I thought. Then I realized I knew the voice. I turned to look, and there she was, running up behind me. Hannah again! I didn't know whether to wait, or to run off and leave her. If I ran, she might go back and tell, so I waited. Her face shone in the heat, from running.

"I saw you sneak away. Where are you going, Paul?"

"Nowhere you need to worry about. Don't you ever mind

your own business?"

"You aren't running away, are you?"

"What if I am? Do you think you're my guardian angel?"

"Do you need someone to watch over you?" she asked, saucily.

"No."

"Good, because I'm nobody's angel." She was staring again, like she could read my mind.

I stared back. This time I noticed the fine features of her face, small-boned and delicate with a straight, narrow nose. Was that what made her eyes so remarkable—their contrast to the smallness of her face? Maybe she wasn't an angel, but she reminded me of a doll I had seen once at the home of a wealthy machinery salesman. The doll had a face of delicate porcelain, with big eyes that closed when you tipped it back. I felt like asking Hannah to look at the clouds so I could see if her eyes closed when she leaned her head back.

"A better friend," she said, breaking the silence.

"A better friend what?" I asked. I had lost the thread of conversation.

"I'm a better *friend* than angel. Do you have anything against friendship?"

"Real friendship is not something you decide on," I replied, swirling the dust with my toe. "Look, I like you fine, but I have to go. I hope you won't mention that you saw me." I started walking away, but she followed.

"Paul, you can't just run away. How will you take care of yourself?"

Did she never give up? "I am not running away," I sighed. "I have to go home to Hutterdorf first. That's all."

"But the train to Germany goes in the morning. What if you are late? If you miss the train, you will be here alone."

"I'm alone anyway. I don't care." I wondered if they would leave me. I hadn't thought about that before. Sannah Basel

would probably be glad to wash her hands of me. I only reminded her how much better her own son used to be. Anyway, it didn't matter. I wanted that box.

"If I miss it, I miss it," I said, increasing my stride.

"What is so important that you have to go back?" she
asked.

I had never seen anyone so nosy. I decided the only way to
get rid of her was to tell her about Mueter's little treasure
box. I kept walking as I talked. "The only place it could be,"
I finished, "is somewhere in the house. I won't go to America
without at least having a look. So I would appreciate it if you
wouldn't tell anybody."

"It's okay," she replied. Her voice was soft with under-
standing. "I will not tell a soul."

"Thanks."

"Because I'm going with you."

"Forget that!" I turned to face her. "You are *not* coming
with me."

"Okay, I'm not," she agreed.

"Good."

"But I am going to Hutterdorf," Hannah added. "You can
come with *me* if you like." Her face was determined.

"Are you crazy?"

Now she was walking ahead. "Come if you want to," she
called, "but I'm going."

What could be done with someone like that? I stuck my
chin out. She wasn't going to tell me what to do. "Go ahead
then!" I yelled back. "Have fun in Hutterdorf. If that's how
it is, I'm not going."

It was her turn to be surprised. She turned back to face me.
"What do you mean you're not going? You'd give up that
easily?" I enjoyed the look of confusion on her face.

"I mean I'm not going with *you*," I answered. "But if you
really want to go, you can go with *me*." I could see I wouldn't

change her mind, but at least this way, it might sound like I was still in charge.

Hannah burst out laughing. "Okay, okay," she said, "how about we just go together? And you can lead the way."

"Okay," I sighed. "But you'd better not slow me down."

"Don't worry. And Paul?"

"Yes?"

"It was nice of you to invite me along."

I rolled my eyes. This girl was infuriating.

"So why are we standing here?" she continued. "Don't you think we'd better hurry up?"

Yes, she was definitely infuriating. I started off at a brisk walk. "Just don't blame me if your parents sell you to the Gypsies when they find out you like to wander."

Hannah was a strong walker, and we kept up a quick pace, following the road across the vast empty flatness of the Russian steppe land. Still, it took longer than I had thought to cover the distance. It was hot and dusty, and with two of us sharing my water jar, we could drink only sparingly.

I almost enjoyed having Hannah along. She could be stubborn and determined, but was good company when she wasn't pushing you around.

About halfway to Hutterdorf, another road angled in to join ours, from the Russian town of Oreknov to the west. As I looked that way, something moved behind a patch of grass. The grass was higher than a horse's withers, the kind of grass Fater had said once covered all of the steppe. I nudged Hannah's arm. "Look at that."

"Look at what?"

I pointed. "Over there, through the grass. I think it's a cart."

Hannah stiffened. "Quick, we've got to hide."

"What for?"

"Haven't you heard of robbers? Or worse yet, it might be someone who knows us."

I looked around. "There's nowhere to hide."

"Over here." She caught my hand and pulled me off the road. There was a small bush, thirty feet away. It wasn't much, but we dived behind it, lying as low as we could. Peering through the branches, I saw a man in a two-wheeled cart.

"What if it's a Gypsy?" Hannah said.

"Just stay still." I didn't know much about Gypsies, but I had heard stories about them kidnapping children. The thought hit me that getting kidnapped by Gypsies might be a good way to escape Sannah Basel. But it would be no good for Hannah.

The cart drew close, its dry wheels squealing on the axle like frightened pigs. It was loaded with sticks, and driven by an old man with a wild-looking, stringy white beard. I realized he was no Gypsy.

"What is he?" Hannah whispered. "He looks like a Hutterite, but half crazy." She was right. The man wore a round, black hat like a Hutterite. His coat was black too, but long, hanging down to his ankles as he sat.

Then I knew. "See those spikes of hair hanging down by his ears? He's a Hasidic Jew. My father sold wheat to some once. There are lots of Jews here in the Ukraine."

"I've never seen them before."

"That's because you've never been off the colony."

"As if you are Mister Man-of-the-World," she scoffed.

Suddenly the screeching wheels went silent.

"*Shhh!*" Hannah hissed. The old man was pulling on the reins, and the horse—an old nag that looked as if it might keel over dead at any moment—stopped. The cart was directly across from our hiding place. We froze, trying to look like part of the landscape.

The man was shouting something.

"I can't understand a word," Hannah whispered, so quietly I could barely hear her.

"It's Yiddish," I replied, "their language." The man jabbered on as if he were making a speech to the grass and rocks at the roadside. Then he stopped and cocked his head, as if listening for a reply. His voice rang out sharply, "*Rebyata*—children! Come away from the bush."

My heart leaped into my mouth, and I saw Hannah's body go rigid. The man had switched to Russian. Though we were better with German, we knew some language of our adopted country as well. We had learned it in school.

"*Edeetyeh seuda*—come here! Do you think I am an old blind dog? I have watched you for a half *verst*—mile."

"We could run," Hannah suggested.

But all at once I felt as if I did not care whether he was a crazy man or not. I was going to Hutterdorf, and his horse and cart were pointed the same way. I wanted that box, and I was not about to run off in the opposite direction. "Let's go see what he wants," I said, standing up. "I don't think Jews are so bad."

"Are you crazy?" Hannah replied, grabbing my arm.

"He's the crazy one," I replied. "Didn't you just say so?" I stepped out from behind the bush and walked boldly toward the most astonishing face I had ever seen.

Chapter 10

Crazy Man

I had to give Hannah credit. She had pluck. She was scared to death of being kidnapped, but she stood by me.

"We agreed to travel together," she said simply.

"Don't worry," I said, trying to sound reassuring. "With that black coat and beard he could almost be a Hutterite preacher." Mind you, the black coat was really a caftan, a robe that hung the full length of his body. It was belted together by a dirty white cloth at his waist.

The man pointed a bony finger at me, and his lips curled into a spine-tingling sneer. Suddenly, the last person he reminded me of was a preacher. My courage turned soft.

His nose hooked downward like a beak, and his eyes were hollow, with the piercing glassy look of an eagle's. It wasn't exactly an evil look, but it occurred to me that Hannah might be wrong about his being *half-crazy*. He looked completely crazy to me.

"*Oh dah*—oh yes—what is this?" he asked, with a voice that rasped like a file on a sheet of tin. "Lost children wandering in the desert, yes?" He waited, his head turning from Hannah to me with the jerky quickness of a bird. When neither of us spoke, he laughed—an old cracked laugh—and repeated himself more loudly. "Lost children wandering in the desert, yes?"

"We know where we're going," I stammered.

He laughed even harder and said, "So you know where

you're going? Then you know more than any man who has walked this empty earth. Do you know where this life will take you?"

This life? What a question! How was I to know? America? Across the ocean? With Sannah Basel? Doubt pinched my heart. Familiar landmarks were gone, and I had no idea how my future would turn out.

"Where is it that you are going then?" the old man asked.

I answered sullenly, "I don't know."

"Oh dah, so now you are honest?" He smiled, showing gaps in his mouth where teeth should have been. "Oh dah—dah, dah."

"We are going to Hutterdorf." It was Hannah speaking up, beside me. "Now we must go, thank you."

"Come," she said to me in German. "Let's go." She turned to leave, expecting me to follow.

The old man laughed. "Through Hutterdorf is the way I go. Oh dah, you shall ride with me."

The next thing I knew, though Hannah objected, we were high up on the cart, jostling along behind the plodding old horse. Hannah was crowded onto the seat with the Jew, and I was right behind her, balancing on a pile of sticks that poked and scratched with every bump. The old fellow talked on as endlessly as the squeaking of the wheels. I didn't mind, except that the longer he muttered and laughed, the more I knew he must be crazy.

For some time he mumbled away in Yiddish as if we were not there. From behind, I stared at his earlock of hair. Most Jews I had seen wore it neatly curled and hanging down. His was like a clump of steppe grass pulled out and stuffed under the edge of his hat. Then all at once he turned to me and said in Russian, "To join the army you may be going?"

"We do not believe in the army," I replied. "Besides I am too young."

"Too young? But older than my boys were."

I wondered what he was talking about. "Your boys were in the army?"

"Dah, oh dah," he replied sadly. "Eight and nine years old, they were too."

Now I was sure he was crazy. "How can eight- and nine-year-olds be in the army?"

"Ah, you are young and do not know about the tsar's great plan to make the Jews stop being Jews. Forty years ago—Tsar Nicholas I—such a plan he had for evil. 'Take the twelve-year-olds for the army,' he said, 'so their parents cannot teach them how to be Jews.' So that is what he did, oh dah, and when the parents tried to hide the children in the forest, he sent the *khappers*—the catchers—to hunt them out. Those khappers were rough and did not rest until they had taken as many children as they had come for."

I had never heard anything like this before. The tsar wanted Hutterites to join the army, but at least he had said if we didn't believe in it we could cut trees in the northern forests instead. And the army did not take twelve-year-olds.

"But your boys were eight and nine, not twelve," I replied.

He fixed me with his glittery eyes. There was a frightening emptiness in his look. "*Nyet*—no—not twelve. When the khappers did not catch all they wanted, they came back at night to search the houses. And who can prove the age of a child? They took what they found. My David and my Reuven, ripped from the arms of their mother and carried away in the night. That is how Jews can be treated in Russia. That is how it is for the Lord's chosen people. Everywhere in the world the Jews are chosen for harm. Hated, robbed, turned over to slavery, burned at the stake, driven out. That is what it means to be different—to be a Jew."

The bitterness in the man's voice seemed to turn even the air to acid. I wondered at his words, *God's chosen people.*

Hadn't it been that way for Hutterites too? Didn't we call ourselves a people set apart for God? Many Hutterites had been tortured and killed for their faith. Those were the martyrs the preachers told about so often in church. Did being chosen by God always mean trouble?

The man laughed his raspy laugh again. "And you think you are too young for the army? Watch out for the khappers!"

"We are going to America," I replied. "There are no khappers there."

For a moment a look of hope flashed through the man's eyes. "America. Oh dah, if I were a younger man. . . . Maybe America is better, yes?"

We were quiet then, until Hannah's soothing voice rose above the clatter and squeal of the wagon. "I am sorry about your sons. It must have been hard for you without them. Were they gone a long time?"

"A long time?" he spat, his eyes gone glittery again. "Is *forever* a long enough time?"

"Forever?" Hannah asked.

"Dead," he replied. "Dead. Don't you know forever?"

Forever. That was the word that had been troubling me lately.

"*Nyet*, what would you children know about forever?"

I felt my jaw muscles stiffen. I knew more about it than he thought. It haunted me every day. Maybe Hannah was innocent, but I knew about forever. That was how long dear Mueter and Fater would be gone. It was a long, empty time.

The old man was talking again. "The Russian army. What could they do with eight-year-olds? Even they did not know, but they found an answer. Oh, they did, and later their answer came back to us in the villages.

"Do you wonder what they did?" he asked. "They marched our army of children into the mountains—a hundred miles. Eating soldier biscuits, and still losing their baby teeth, they were. Wearing old soldier coats and walking through mud and cold, mile after mile into the teeth of the wind. And what do you think? A third of them died. So they turned around and marched them back again, and half of those died. Is that how a country treats its children?" The man was angry now. His knotted beard shook on his jaw like a magpie nest on a wind-blown branch. He stamped a foot on the wagon board. His fist punched the air, his elbow bumping Hannah. She moved closer to the edge of the seat.

Then suddenly his crazy laugh burst from his lips again like a ragged cough. "Did anyone know where they were marching?" he said. "Oh dah, they were marching to the grave. So there was my Reuven, gentle Reuven, coughing his life out at the side of the road, and little David, the younger but always the stronger, refusing to leave him."

He quit talking. I looked at Hannah. Her face was white with feeling. Her eyes shone with fright or held-in tears, I did not know which. Then she turned to him and said, "I'm sorry, sir, to hear it. It was a terrible thing." Her voice was like the brush of a soothing hand.

But the old man was in no mind to be soothed. He looked from Hannah to me with a terrifying gleam of red madness in his eyes. He was full of danger. Fear pricked my scalp. But I was curious too.

"Did they leave them there on the road?" I asked.

"Hah!" he shouted. "Did they leave them on the road? What a question you should ask. Oh dah, they left them on the road. But not until the army man sticks my little David with a knife because he will not march! Such is life for the Jew.

"And should it be any different for children such as you?" he raved. "Stuck like a baked potato on a knife!" Suddenly, he reached inside his caftan, and his hand came out holding a long blade. Turning toward Hannah, he raised his arm in the air.

"Hannah, look out!" I cried. Scrambling up from the sticks, I leaped to shove Hannah from the bench, but she had already jumped. Right behind her, I hit the ground running. Expecting the stab of a knife blade at any second, we ran like twin tornadoes, a blur of dust whirling at our heels.

Chapter 11

The Treasure Box

Anyone who says girls can't run never saw Hannah running from that Jew. We both ran faster than a jackrabbit. In my mind, I pictured the old man whipping his horse to a gallop, his glittering eagle eyes aiming the knife point straight at our backs. But I heard no pounding hooves, and the squealing wagon wheels did not change their sound.

Looking back, I was surprised to see him sitting high on the cart, laughing insanely. We stopped. Instead of chasing us, he was holding a burlap sack open beside him. I had seen it when we were on the cart. The knife was still in the air, but now there was a big potato stuck on the point. He opened his mouth and bit a piece off.

Waving the knife, he shouted, "*Rebyata*—children, God will repay. God always repays!" Pieces of potato fluttered like snow from his mouth as he laughed his mad, raspy laugh.

"He's crazy as a half-plucked rooster," I said to Hannah as we turned to go.

"He's a bitter and hurting old man. It's horrible what happened to his children," she said, looking into me with her big brown eyes. "If only he could turn to God for healing."

Hutterdorf was not more than a mile away, so we jogged the rest of the way to keep well ahead of the crazy old man. Along the way, I couldn't escape the feeling that Hannah had been telling me something. The Jew was a bitter old man who had never allowed God to heal his pain over the loss of his children. Did she think I was like him because I had lost my parents? A shudder went through me. Had I just seen a picture of myself in another fifty years? Hannah probably thought I needed God to heal me. But she didn't know the whole story. Besides, if God really wanted to help me, he wouldn't have turned me over to Sannah Basel's care. Maybe the old man was right. God always repays. *Is this what it's like to be in God's bad books?* I wondered.

Instead of entering Hutterdorf by the street, I led us through pastures at the village edge. I didn't want to meet adults who might ask questions. There was probably no need to worry. So many Hutterdorfers were leaving for America, they would be too busy to pay attention to us.

We crept to the back of the house through the orchard trees and around the attached barn. I had no desire to see the front yard, with its gate and terrible memories.

As I had guessed, the window shutters were closed tight, but the back door had no lock. It opened easily, and we slipped into the dark winter-kitchen.

Digging candles out of my bag, I gave one to Hannah. I lit it with a match, and a halo of light spread around us. With another candle I touched her flame, receiving a light for myself.

The shock took my breath away. The room was bare. I had known it would be, yet I wasn't prepared for the empty house. In my memories, it was still so full of life. My heart sank. Andreas Vetter was right. There was nothing to rummage through, nowhere for a box to be misplaced.

Doubt clouded Hannah's face, and I knew she was thinking the same thing.

"Well, why are we standing here? Let's get looking," I said, with annoyance. Hannah said nothing, but began walking about with her candle. We searched, holding our lights to empty cupboards and dark corners of the rooms—the kitchen, the living room with the stove, the bedroom I had slept in all of my life, Mueter and Fater's bedroom, and even the attic where the grain had been stored. The whole time, I wanted to cry from the loneliness of the empty house. I stayed away from Hannah, in case a stray tear gleamed in the candlelight.

At last, we tried the summer room again. It, too, should have been a bedroom, but with no other children, Mueter had furnished it with a desk, a chair, and a lamp. She called it her *klana Welt*—little world. It was where she came to write, and sometimes read. If the box were anywhere, it would be here. But we could see only bare walls and ceiling. I slumped to the floor. What was the use? Tomorrow we would leave for America, and what would I have to take with me? Nothing! And Sannah Basel would be spitting nails, she would be so angry.

I flopped back to lie on the floor, but hit my head on the wall instead. The pain jerked my arm, and I tipped the candle, spilling hot wax on my hand. Yelping angrily, I slammed the wall with my fist. A spasm shot up my arm. I'd nearly broken my knuckles. "Stupid," I muttered. "Everything I do is stupid."

Hannah reached down to put her hand on my arm. "Don't touch me!" I yelled. "Just mind your own business for a change!"

"Fine!" she shot back. "Keep to your stubborn self, if that's what you want." She backed off and stood by the door. "I'm sorry about the box," she added, more gently.

"Don't bother." I felt the energy draining from my body, and almost cried. But I felt the tears coming, and laughed instead, to stop them. "I hope you liked the house tour," I joked. "Wasn't it fun?" I laughed again, but my laughter sounded hollow. It reminded me of the crazy old Jew. I shut up quick. Was his crazy laugh just something that kept him from crying?

"Sorry for snapping at you," I offered quietly. "We might as well go."

I slid my hand along the floor to get up. "Hey!" I said. "What's this?" One board had moved a little.

Hannah was right down beside me. "A short board," she said. It was only about a foot long.

"Mueter always had a rug right here." I took Fater's knife from my pocket and caught the edge of the board with the point. The board lifted smoothly from the floor, revealing a small cubbyhole underneath.

"The box!" Hannah cried, holding her candle to the chamber. "That must be the box."

"No wonder I hardly ever saw it," I cried. I could hardly believe my mother had a secret chamber. It seemed more like something for a king or a pirate than a Hutterite woman.

I reached in and pulled out the wooden box. There was a picture of a cigar on it, and Russian writing. The box was tied shut with a leather thong. Holding my breath, I untied it and opened the lid.

Inside was a book—my precious Mueter's diary. There was also a small brass cross, about two inches tall, attached to a gold chain. It surprised me that my Hutterite mother had owned such an object. But what really made my eyes pop was what I saw on top of the book. Folded neatly, and held down by the cross, was a stack of brand-new, crisp, Russian money.

Chapter 12
Over the Edge

Hannah and I stared at the bills.

"What do you know, Paul? Real treasure," she breathed.

"In Mueter's little treasure box." Money was the last thing I had expected to find. The cubbyhole must have been my parents' safe place to keep extra farming money. I looked at Hannah. "They were going to buy machinery from farmers going to America. This must be the money for it."

"How much is there?" Hannah wondered.

With shaking hands, I took it out. We counted it together, as I laid the bills on the floor. There were 500 rubles.

"What will you do with it?"

"I don't know." There was enough money to sail five or six times to America.

"I can tell you one thing. Sannah Basel won't get it." I stuffed the bills into my deep pants pocket. Communal Hutterites were not supposed to keep money for themselves. Sannah would only give it to the colony. They had gotten the money for everything my family had owned. This money would be mine. I would hide it somehow, and use it to go out on my own someday.

I glared sternly at Hannah. "Will you promise not to tell anyone?"

She glared right back. "What's it to me? It's your money." She hesitated, then grinned. "Of course, if you let me hold that wad for a minute, you could be more sure of my loyalty."

I sighed and pulled it out of my pocket. "Here you are. Just don't go running away from me now."

Hannah fingered the bills. "I just wondered what it feels like. I've never had more than twenty-five kopecks to buy a few candies."

While Hannah held the money, I looked at the little cross. I had never seen it before. It was the sort of thing owned by many Russians of the Orthodox Church, but most Hutterites would consider it a graven image, forbidden by the Bible.

Looking more closely, I realized that the bottom corner and one end of the crosspiece were beveled and fixed with hinges. I pressed a small button on the other side, and the cross opened in the middle. I gasped when I looked inside. Hannah looked over my shoulder.

There were two little photographs, one on each side—Mueter and Fater! They were much younger than I remembered, but there was no mistaking them. There was Fater's strong chin and straight sloping nose. And Mueter's kind eyes, and curving lips that looked as if she knew something amusing that everyone else had missed. I held the cross reverently in my hands.

"It's lovely," Hannah murmured.

"I can't believe they had this," I said. Even to most non-communal Hutterites, photographs and crosses were as bad as idol worship.

"I bet they got it when they fell in love," Hannah sighed. "I think it shows their love for each other, nestled in the bosom of the cross."

She had a dreamy look in her eyes. *Typical girl*, I thought, *making it sound so romantic*. But maybe she was right. My parents had certainly loved one another, and they always put Christ at the center of their lives.

"They must have been special people," Hannah said, softly.

"They were," was all I could answer. There was a lump in my throat, and also the stab of guilt. They were gone, and there was no changing what I had done.

Hannah returned the money. I put it back in my pocket, then tied the cigar box shut. I would have to read the diary another time. Now we had to hurry back. Still, I insisted on visiting the cemetery before we left, and by the time we got out on the road the sun was almost down.

It was the darkest night I could remember. From down the road not a glimmer of light showed in the sky. There was no moon, and clouds covered the stars. We managed to stay on the road by feeling the grass at the edge brush our clothes. When it brushed on the right, we moved to the left; when it brushed on the left, we moved to the right. It was slow going.

We tried walking by candle flame, but worrisome breezes kept puffing them out. Besides, who knew if robbers or gypsies, or even our old Jewish friend might be out on the road? We felt safer in the darkness.

Once, I heard a rustle and a thud as Hannah fell in the grass. At the same moment my foot went into a hole, and I got a face full of dirt when I landed. When I jumped up to see if Hannah was all right, I rammed my nose right into her forehead. "Ouch!" I yelled, grabbing my nose.

"Hey!" she cried. I heard her tumble to the ground again. "Can't you watch where you're going?"

"Watch where I'm going? As if *you* can see in the dark," I said, sarcastically.

"At least I'm not running around with my head stuck out like a goose," she grumbled.

"No," I said, "you'd rather sneak around like a ghost in a graveyard." She had a lot of nerve.

Suddenly, Hannah's fingers brushed my arm—then her hand slid down to grasp mine.

"Here," Hannah said, "maybe this will work better. At

least we can keep track of each other."

For a moment I drew back, but a thrill of emotion rushed through me. All I could think was, *She is a girl*, as if I hadn't noticed before. I forced the thought from my mind. I didn't want to hold hands with anyone.

But then again, I reasoned, *it is a dark night.* Maybe Hannah was scared. I squeezed her hand. It was small and warm.

It was strange, walking in the dark like that, almost like floating, where the road was smooth. In the privacy of blindness, the little hand in mine was strangely comforting. It was almost like a dream where everything was good again. I started to relax.

"You see," Hannah said, "it's easier together than alone, don't you think?"

"I guess so," I replied. Why argue if it made her feel better? "I'm sorry I took so long at the cemetery. Your mother will be fit to be tied."

"We're both in for it, sure. Your Basel won't be too happy."

That was an understatement. She'd be breathing fire. "The dragon lady can be unhappy if she wants," I said. "It's nothing to me. But your parents will think I'm a troublemaker, too."

"Maybe, but I think they'll understand. They want me to be your friend."

My hand went rigid in hers. "Is that why you've been hanging around? Because your *parents* want you to?" What an idiot I had been to enjoy her company!

"No," she said. "It was my own idea. When I saw you at the funeral, I thought you could use a friend. And now that I've got to know you, I've decided I like being with you."

I let go of her hand. That was even worse—hanging around because she felt sorry for me. "Oh, sure," I said sarcastically, "do pity projects make you feel good? Well, I don't need your good deeds."

"The trouble with you, Paul," she answered hotly, "is that

you've got a wall around you, and you won't let it down for a minute. Why won't you let anyone touch you? Do you *want* to keep hurting?"

"And you think you have the magic touch, right? Don't bother yourself, Hannah. You're not my healer."

"No, but Jesus could be if you'd let him."

Now I was really bugged. This colony girl didn't have to tell me about Jesus. "What Jesus are you talking about? I don't see anything around the Gemein but rules. Do you think having twenty-five bosses and obeying rules for everything makes Jesus love you more?"

"Is that what you think?" Hannah asked, with ice in her voice. "That I only care about rules? I'm not exactly obeying the rules being here with you, am I? But guess what? Jesus loves me anyway. You don't like the way we live, and you won't look past that to see the good. You're not used to it, but it's the same God here that you worshiped before. It's the same God your mother and father worshiped too." She stopped talking and I could hear the soft shuffle of our steps on the dirt road. I stayed stubbornly silent.

"It doesn't matter what you think of me," Hannah continued, "but don't turn your back on God just because you don't like the way I live."

I didn't have to listen to her. I stuck my nose in the air and sniffed, trying to look snooty, which was silly, since she couldn't see me anyway. But when I sniffed, I noticed that the air smelled fresher than it had before.

"Paul, I know it's been hard on you. You miss your parents. But don't shut out everyone else."

I couldn't stand it anymore. "They weren't *your* parents. You don't know anything about it."

"No, Paul, they weren't my parents. But don't think you're the only one who ever felt any pain."

"And what's your biggest heartache?" I asked sarcastically.

"Forget it!" She was really mad now.

"Fine."

"You're so stubborn you wouldn't hear it any—"

I heard a bump and Hannah cried, "Oww!" Then there was a thud, and . . . nothing.

"Hannah? Hannah!" I called, "What happened?" There was no answer. Then it sounded like I was walking on wood. All of a sudden I was scared. "Hannah?" I said, feeling my way over to where her voice had been. I bumped my shin on something hard. I reached out with my hands. It was some kind of a log rail. I tried to climb over and almost went head over heels. My leg was dangling into empty space.

Chapter 13
Hannah's Story

I scrambled frantically to my hands and knees, groping in the dark. Where was I? And what had happened to Hannah? I must be on a bridge, and Hannah must have fallen over the edge. But how could that be? There was no bridge on this road.

I followed the rail, all my anger forgotten. I should never have been arguing with Hannah. What if she were dead? Did everybody I touched have to die? Why had I let her come?

Then I heard a groan. Thank God! I scrambled in the direction of the voice, tumbling down a dirt bank and across a flat of soft, sandy earth. My hand splashed into water. A stream. That's why the air had smelled so fresh. I crawled beside it, reaching ahead of me. My hands came down on something cloth-covered and soft. Hannah! I shook her gently. *Ach, Himble*—heaven! I jerked away. It was her backside I was shaking! *Ei yi yi,* what a thing to do! She would think I was perverted.

"I'm sorry," I blubbered foolishly. "I didn't mean . . . Hannah! Hannah, talk to me."

"What? Paul? What happened?"

"Thank goodness. Are you all right? You fell off a bridge. We're in a creek bed."

"A bridge? Where? Oh-h, my head hurts."

I dug into my bag for a candle. I lit it, cupping my hand

around it as a shield from the breeze. Hannah sat up slowly, holding a hand to her forehead. Her dark kerchief had slipped, revealing the rolls of hair pulled back behind her ears. Blood seeped between her fingers.

"Your forehead is really bleeding." I took out the handkerchief that had been wrapped around the candles and folded it crookedly with one hand. In my other hand I held the candle, shielded by my body. "Press this handkerchief on the cut."

"Your handkerchief? Maybe—"

"Don't worry," I interrupted. "I didn't blow my nose in it." I couldn't blame her for wondering. Almost everybody carried a nose-blowing handkerchief.

"Can you see me okay?" I asked.

"My forehead is bleeding, not my eyes," she answered.

"Head injuries can make things look fuzzy. Can you see okay?"

"Fine."

"Good." I took off my coat and dipped the end of one sleeve into the creek water. I wiped the blood from her face, then held the handkerchief to her forehead so she could wash her hands in the water. She dried them on her apron.

"Now what are we going to do?" Hannah asked. "And where did this creek come from? I don't remember any creek."

"No," I agreed. "But there is one on the road to Oreknov. I don't know how we did it, but we must have angled off our road where it meets this one. You can't tell which way you're going in this darkness."

She nodded. "Maybe it happened when we bumped into each other before we . . ." I was glad she stopped without finishing "before we held hands." Instead she said, "We'll be terribly late now. We'd better get going."

We rose to leave, but before we could climb out of the creek bed, she sat down. "Oh, my head—it hurts to move."

The walk would be longer than ever now, but I realized

Hannah couldn't spend the night stumbling around in the dark, holding a handkerchief to her throbbing head. "Maybe we'd better rest for a while," I suggested.

"Just for a bit," she agreed.

I gathered some dead branches that had caught on the bridge, then climbed out of the gully to get an armload of dry grass. I built a fire by a little hollow in the bank where it could not be seen from out on the steppe.

We sat staring into the fire. I whittled at a stick with Fater's knife. "How does your head feel now?" I asked Hannah after a while.

"It throbs, but I think it has quit bleeding."

"Should I take a look at it?"

Hannah smiled. "The cloth is stuck to my head."

"Well, don't pull it away. It might start bleeding again. Maybe you should tie it on with your kerchief."

"Can you help?"

I untied her kerchief from under her chin. It was not proper for a Hutterite girl to take it off outdoors, but this was necessary. Besides, she still had her *Mitz*, the small cloth undercap. Seeing her hair like that in the firelight reminded me for a moment of my mother's, except that Hannah's was shiny chestnut brown instead of blond. I tied the kerchief around her head. "You look like a wounded soldier from the Crimean War," I laughed.

"Do you think I'll get a hero's welcome for coming home alive?"

"If your parents don't skin you for worrying them to death." I wasn't looking forward to our return. Tomorrow was Friday. I knew the people were planning to leave for Alexandrovsk at nine o'clock in the morning to catch the train. We still had plenty of time to get back, but there would be an uproar over this.

"You must wish you had never come along, Hannah."

"Well, I'm glad I got to help you find those things in the box, but I guess I slowed you down after all. I'm sorry."

I shrugged. "Ah, Hannah, you're a pain, but I enjoyed your company."

"All of it?"

"Well, maybe not all—"

"Look, Paul, I know you didn't like the things I said about asking Jesus for help and not shutting everyone out. But you were wrong to say I don't know anything about it."

I sighed. She would not give up. But short of strangling her, what could I do? I listened.

"Do you remember, three years ago, about Peter Dekker?"

Black shadows from the firelight danced on Hannah's face. The name didn't sound familiar. I shrugged. "No. What about him?"

"It was in a sawmill at Sheromet. He was killed."

I thought for a while. Yes, it did stir a memory. Fater had come home one night telling about a man who got caught in the carriage of a sawmill. The man's head was crushed like a watermelon. I wondered what Hannah was getting at. "I remember. It was a terrible accident."

Hannah's throat was tight when she spoke. "Well, Peter Dekker was my father."

My jaw fell open. No wonder she always looked at me like she understood my feelings. "I . . . I didn't know" was all I could say.

"They told me you saw it happen," Hannah continued, "to your parents, I mean—in the storm. Well, I was there, too, when *my* father died. It was horrible." Her voice was shaky, but her eyes were strong as she looked at me through the flickering light.

"For a long time I thought I wanted to die too. Everything was dark and empty without Fater. I hated that time. Only Mueter saved me. It was horrible for her, too, but she trusted

God's love, and helped me see that what happened didn't mean God had quit loving me."

So Hannah knew the pain of losing a parent, too—of being left alone by someone who loved her. Of course, she did not carry my guilt, but even so, I wondered how she could be so contented. "I'm sorry about your father, Hannah."

"Thanks."

"Still, it's different for me."

"I know. I have Mueter. And now my stepfather loves me like a real father. Your Vetter is kind, but it can't be easy living with your Sannah Basel."

"I would rather live in a lion's den," I agreed.

"She wasn't always so hard, you know. They say she changed when her Daniel died of pneumonia."

"*Joh*, I know. Mueter used to say the sun rose and set on Sannah's golden boy."

"Paul," Hannah said, her brown eyes boring holes in me again, "don't become like your Basel. Let someone be your friend."

The breeze had died down. The night was warm, but a chill went up my spine. *Don't be like your Basel*. Did Hannah think I was that bad? If only I could be happy again. But how could I? At least Hannah still had her mother. But it was more than that. She had not killed her father. How was I supposed to ask Jesus for help when I had turned him against me? And what kind of love did Jesus show anyway, to answer a prayer that way? Didn't he know I never would have traded my parents for America? I wanted the wrong thing, so he gave it to me and took everything else away! *Forget it Hannah*, I thought. *I won't ask him for anything again*.

I could see that Hannah was hurting. And she looked tired. "You should sleep," I said, to avoid more conversation.

"Sure, just for a bit."

"When it's light we can cut across the steppe to the other

road. It will be shorter."

"That's good. But Paul, do you think—"

"*Joh*, Hannah, I'll think about it," I lied, just to get her off my back. What a strange person she was. I gave her my bag for a pillow, and my jacket for a blanket. "Your head will feel better when you wake up."

Soon she was asleep. I threw more wood on the fire, and sat close to its light with Mueter's box. Then I took out the diary, and opened it to see if my mother would speak.

Chapter 14

It Must Be Burned!

Looking at Mueter's neatly formed German letters, I could almost see her hand holding the pen and carefully dipping it in the inkbottle. I lingered over the vision of her thoughtful face, her green eyes looking into the far-off place where she collected the words for her writing.

As I paged through the diary, my name jumped out at me from one of the longer passages. It was dated 1862, not long after I was born. I leaned closer to the fire to read.

> *Dear Lord, I think of my Paul, giving thanks to you for this boy, this gift of a child. Perhaps there will be no more, as the doctor thinks. If so, grant me your contentment and peace. I ask also for wisdom that my husband and I may train him to love you. Let him trust you and obey you. It is my prayer that he will always walk in your truth and your love. What more could a mother ask?*

Reading my mother's words was almost like touching her gentle hand, or hearing her voice, they were so peaceful. I could always count on Mueter to make a hard thing sound easy, or a bad thing seem good.

But something else burned inside me when I read the words, something bitter. Love. It stung like pickle vinegar in a cut. How could I love when the ones I loved were gone? Did God mock me even with my own mother's wisdom?

I stared into the fire, clutching the book to my chest. I would read the rest of it later.

I must have fallen asleep, because the next thing I knew I was lifting my head from the ground. The fire was out. I was shocked to see the sun already high in the sky. *Ei yi!* We would have to hurry now. Everyone would be leaving soon for the train.

I shook Hannah awake, careful to touch only her shoulder.

Hannah felt much better after sleeping, and soon we were angling southwest across the steppe, toward the Sheromet road. Though her head still throbbed, she trudged along without complaining. I worried about what her mother would think when she saw her rumpled clothes and my bloody handkerchief on her head.

It must have taken over an hour to get back to the right road. "I wonder what time it is," Hannah said.

"I don't know. If we're lucky, we'll get back before they're ready to leave."

"I just hope we don't meet them on the way."

That was when we saw a wagon coming from the direction of Hutterdorf. It was too late to hide.

"Maybe it's our crazy friend again," Hannah smiled nervously. "I thought we were going to get stabbed."

"Just try not to look like a potato," I joked. "Anyway, it's a four-wheeled wagon."

The wagon turned out to be a Hutterite wagon. It was someone from a neighboring colony. When I heard what he said, I almost wished it had been the old Jewish man again.

"Hello, *Kinder*—children. Paul and Hannah, would you be? The whole countryside has been looking for you."

● ● ●

"It is after nine o'clock!" Her eyes were blocks of ice that could have frozen my insides had my own hot rebellion not burned against her gaze. Sannah Basel stood tall and rigid in the crowd gathered around our wagon. Her lips were a thin white line across her face.

By the time Hannah and I had arrived at the colony, we had met several searchers on horseback. Our wagon driver told us sternly that the people had already left for Alexandrovsk to catch the train. They'd had no choice. It was a four-hour wagon trip, with baggage to unload and tickets to arrange before the four o'clock departure.

Sannah and Andreas and Hannah's family had stayed behind. All the neighboring Hutterites and Mennonites who were not using their wagons to haul people and luggage to the train station had gathered to help with the search. Teams of searchers walked the fields surrounding the Gemein. The man we rode with had been all the way to Hutterdorf, while others checked the road south.

After we arrived, the searchers straggled in. Anger pinched the faces of some, while relief softened others.

Suddenly a small woman came running from the edge of the colony. It was Hannah's mother. Her face looked tired, and her eyes, brown like Hannah's, were red-rimmed from crying. She threw her arms around her daughter and cried some more. "*Ach, mah Lieba*—my love—what has happened?" she asked fingering the bloodied handkerchief.

Our wagon driver related what we had told him, and we tried to explain the rest.

Then I stood stiff-backed as Sannah lashed me with her tongue. "I do not know why we ever agreed to take you under our roof. Such rebellion! You have defied me and run off. You have almost ruined the entire move to America! What is wrong with you? Why can you not be more like . . . like other boys your age?"

I knew what she'd been going to say—Why couldn't I be like her Daniel? I was going to tell her how I'd hate to be like anyone she would love, when Hannah intervened.

"It is my fault too. We expected to be back last night, but it was terribly dark. I fell off a bridge and hit my head, and Paul had no choice but to stay with me. I am so sorry."

"Well *he* is not sorry," Sannah said, pointing a finger at me. "As if sorry would make it right." She breathed a deep sigh that sounded like the hiss of a snake.

I could have spit hot rivets, she made me so angry, but I swallowed my pride. "I *am* sorry, Sannah Basel. I'm sorry for the trouble I caused."

"Sorry?" she retorted. "Smug is what you are."

I squared my shoulders. "I am sorry for the trouble I caused, but not that I found the box," I said, holding it in front of me. "You said it wasn't there, but you're too much of an old ogre to admit you were wrong."

Sannah's face went white. Quick as a snake, she snatched the box from my hands. "A boy like you does not deserve to keep such a thing."

"Give it back!"

Sannah opened the box. She pulled out the cross, staring in disbelief. "God forbid! A graven image. Can a Hutterite keep an idol?" She fumbled with the catch, and the cross popped open. "With photographs inside!" she gasped. "Ungodly! It must be burned."

"Do not burn it, Sannah Basel."

"Such things are not for the godly."

"Give it back!"

"Enough!" she cried.

Then I lost control. The thought of Sannah Basel burning Mueter's little cross with the pictures inside was more than I could bear. I looked at her through flames of hate. "Thief!" I cried. "You stole everything I have, and now you want this!"

"Does Satan twist your heart? Is giving you a home stealing from you?"

"Give back the box, poison woman!" I screamed.

My words stopped everything. The accusing stares of the people said, *Does Sannah deserve such a rebellious child? Is the boy out of his mind?* It was something I was beginning to wonder myself. My whole world was out of order.

Then things got worse. Around the corner of the wagon came old Graybeard with a willow switch in his hand. It was his job to punish me for causing so much trouble. He had arrived just in time to hear me shouting at Sannah. His face was grim.

Chapter 15

Graybeard's Switch

Goose grease. The Hutterite cure-all. It was used for all skin problems, including cuts, scrapes, boils, and rashes. Both Hannah and I were wearing it—she on her forehead, I on my backside.

Hannah had taken a switching from old Graybeard too, but she was already suffering from the gash on her head, so the teacher went easy on her.

As for me, I got the licking of my life. After all, I was the one who had "led Hannah astray" with my rebellion. I was the one who had shouted at Sannah as if the devil had hold of my tongue. Graybeard took me behind the barn, where he made me bend over, with my hands on the rough boards, as he swatted away with a willow switch.

"As I told you before," he said, "this is not for my pleasure. It is for your good. 'Train a child in the way he should go, and when he is old he will not turn from it.' "

The willow switch whistled in the air and sent a blistering red flash from my backside to my brain. "To live in community you must learn not to be self-willed." *Whoosh*! Another hot brand seared me.

"You have ignored the wishes of your Basel and Vetter." *Smack*! The stick burned me again. "You have led Hannah into disobedience." *Swack*! The switch whistled and sang on my tender skin. "And you have tempted the sinful nature by spending the entire night with her alone." *Spang*! Another blow. But this time his words stung worse than the switch.

I spat out, "It's nothing like that, you nasty old—"

Smack! The switch cut off my words, and I bit my tongue in pain.

"Perhaps it was nothing, but you must learn your place. If everyone did as he pleased, we Hutterites could not live together in harmony. The community always comes first." *Swack*! He blistered me again, then gave me several more licks for good measure.

The *discussion* was over—not that I tried to talk any more. I had almost yelped when the switch caught me with my first mouthful of words. I couldn't risk crying, so I kept my mouth clamped shut.

Yes, old Graybeard knew how to use a willow switch as well as a strap. The only good thing was that he had let me keep my pants on, though the cloth did little to lessen the pain. A few minutes later, when Andreas Vetter came around with the jar of goose grease, my pants did come down.

"Paul, *mah* Paul," he said, as if he were hurting too, "what is to become of you? You have such a stubborn will." He smeared a glob of goose grease on the welts that were already rising. It felt cool. "This time you deserved to be punished," he continued, screwing the lid back on the jar. "Now pull up your trousers, and let's go." He put his hand on my shoulder as if trying to be fatherly. Then he added, "You were right about the box." I stiffened. What good was that, if Sannah burned it?

Tobias Tschetter, a Hutterite from another colony, waited with a wagon to take us to Alexandrovsk. With shouts and confusion, we rushed away to catch the train. *Trust Graybeard to risk being late just for the chance to strap me*, I thought, bitterly.

Hannah had a seven-year-old brother and two sisters,

four-year-old Maria and one-year-old Barbara. The wagon was crowded with her family, as well as Tobias, Graybeard, Sannah, Andreas, and me—not to mention our luggage. Hannah's brother Checkela bounced around like one of the lopsided bladder balls we used for kicking games.

Sannah and Andreas took the first turn up on the high wagon seat with Tobias, while everyone else sat on suitcases and boxes. The teacher made a point of staying between Hannah and me, keeping us apart. Lying on my stomach to protect my burning welts, I kept to the back of the wagon and pretended not to care. Sahra Stahl fussed over Hannah, straightening her hair, checking her bandaged forehead, patting her shoulder. She was overjoyed to have her daughter back. I couldn't help but envy my partner in crime.

I hated Graybeard for what he had suggested about my staying with Hannah through the night. I imagined myself setting him straight. *If I did even one thing improper with Hannah*, I argued self-righteously, *May God strike me dead!* Then I remembered my hand on her backside, and instantly regretted the thought. With my luck, God might take me up on my challenge. But I almost didn't care. At least I'd be out of here.

● ● ●

The wagon ride was a lesson in agony. The driver pushed the horses as hard as he could to make up for lost time. The wagon was meant for hauling grain, not people. Every bump jounced and jarred me among the trunks and boxes, banging my ribs and hipbones. I yearned to change position, to kneel or sit, but touching anything with my tender backside was out of the question. It felt like a pincushion stuck full of hot needles.

It seemed every time I wished for something, I got it with a vengeance. One moment I was bouncing along, wishing to get off the wagon and lie on a nice piece of soft ground. The next moment I was tumbling in a confusion of boxes, dust, and shouts of surprise.

We were on a smooth stretch of road, making good time, when suddenly the wagon bucked violently sideways. I heard the crack of splitting wood, and the whole back end of the wagon fell with a crash to the ground. The trunk I was lying on bounced off into the dirt, sending me somersaulting and skidding to a stop on my pincushion rump.

I might have howled like a baby, except that what happened next made me want to howl with laughter. I had a perfect view of Hannah and her family tumbling off after me, bouncing and rolling on the road. Amazingly, Hannah's mother came to rest on her back, holding little Barbara safely in the air above her. Checkela, bouncing for real now, ended up sitting, bewildered and rubbing dust from his eyes, beside the four-year-old. Graybeard hung onto the back of the wagon. He had a death grip on the sides, and his dragging feet scrabbled for traction, skittering behind him like duck feet stirring a pond.

But the best part was just beginning. Frightened by the crash, the horses lit out down the road. As the wagon jerked ahead, Sannah Basel bowled over backward from the seat into the tipped-down wagon box. Legs and arms whirling like windmill blades, skirts flying over her head like a black sail, she slid down the wagon bed, head over heels, right into Graybeard! Graybeard lost his grip, and the two of them tumbled over each other like mixed-up leap-froggers. They landed in a tangle on the road.

Through the dust I saw the driver and Andreas Vetter hanging on to the wagon seat for dear life, their unbuttoned black coats flapping behind them as the horses ran.

I had no idea what had happened, but looking behind me,

I saw the back wheels, axle and all, rolling to a stop by the edge of the road. The axle and wheels had bounced from under the end of the wagon, leaving nothing to hold it up. A pole stuck out from the middle of the axle. The *reach* had broken in half.

Scuffling and muttering sounds drew my attention back to Sannah and the teacher. They were sprawled in a heap. Sannah, lying on top of Graybeard, thrashed about like a pig in a gunnysack, her apron tangled over her head.

"*Ach, Himble*—heaven!" she shouted, trying to untangle herself.

"Help me!" Graybeard gasped, wriggling like a worm to get free. "I'm choking!"

Suddenly he gave a mighty shove, bouncing Sannah to the ground, and rolled himself away. Sannah's head popped into the daylight from under her apron. Sputtering and spitting dirt from her dusty lips, she jumped to her feet. But she was standing on her own skirt. There was a loud ripping sound, and she fell again, sitting in a heap. Sannah quit fighting then, and sat still, looking dazedly around. Finally her gaze rested on me. She glared. "There, Paul," she said grimly, "now see what you've done with your running away."

Me again. Who else could have caused the wagon to break apart?

Graybeard picked himself up and stumbled quickly to my Basel.

"Sannah, are you hurt?" he asked, reaching shakily for her hands. "Let me help you." He lifted her to her feet, and almost dropped her in the same motion. "You've taken a nasty tum—" Graybeard choked on his words as Sannah's skirt parted where it had ripped and slipped down past her knees. A billow of white underthings greeted our eyes, freezing us all in astonishment.

Chapter 16
Sannah's Pain

I will never forget the picture of Graybeard and Sannah Basel. They stood in the middle of the road, Graybeard holding Sannah's arms, and her skirt hanging around her knees. Graybeard's mouth, wide open in shock, was like a dark cloud in the fiery sunset of his blushing face. I expected him to turn and run, but his feet seemed to have grown roots. Sannah's horrified face was bug-eyed and white, as if a great pressure were squeezing the blood away and trying to pop out her eyes.

I was afraid she might explode. And then she did.

"Let go, *du dummer Mensch*—stupid man!" she screamed. She shook the bewildered Graybeard loose, flailing her arms. She stamped and whirled, shouting, "Get away, go away!" Only when she tripped and nearly fell on her face did she stop and look down at the skirt around her ankles, and see her underskirts fluttering in the breeze. Quickly she bent and yanked up the skirt, tying it wildly with her apron string.

None of the Stahl family even tried to intervene. In fact no one moved at all—only stared in sheepish silence, while Graybeard took refuge behind a trunk.

"What are you looking at?" Sannah shouted to no one in particular. She was gazing up toward the sky. If I hadn't known better, I'd have thought she was yelling at God.

A clattering rattle drew our attention to the returning horses and the wagon dragging behind. Tobias, the driver, walked in front, holding the lines. Andreas hurried to Sannah.

"Are you all right?" he asked, full of concern. He put his hand on Sannah's shoulder.

"Do not touch me," she replied angrily. She pointed at me. "*See* the trouble he has caused with his cigar box, and photographs and graven images. I shall burn them all!"

"Now Sannah—"

"He has been nothing but trouble since he came. And now look what he has done!"

"Sannah, he did not break the wagon," Andreas Vetter replied.

At least *he* was sensible.

"Had he not run away," she retorted, "we would not be here missing our train."

"We will not miss our train. And as for Paul, he has had his punishment. Now we must forgive," Andreas pleaded. "Be easier on him, and let him be a boy."

It seemed the two of them had forgotten about me and the others. They spoke as if alone.

"He is rebellious," Sannah said. "If we must look after him, we will have rules and obedience. We must break his willfulness."

At this, Andreas' voice grew very quiet. "And what of love, Sannah? What of love?"

"Do not tell me about love," Sannah snapped, her voice hard. "Have I not loved? And what was my reward?"

Andreas sighed wearily, lifting his wife's chin with a tender hand. "Sannah, *mah Lieba*—my love—being hard with Paul will not bring our Daniel back."

Suddenly Sannah's bones seemed to melt within her. She collapsed on the ground like a pile of old clothes. Only her shoulders were rigid, as if stiffened by a coat hanger. They shook—with anger, I thought at first. Then I heard sobbing.

Andreas Vetter knelt beside Sannah, trying to comfort her, but she would not stop crying. Sahra, Hannah's mother, wrapped her arms around Sannah, whispering sweetly.

I had often thought I would enjoy seeing Sannah cry—that it would make me feel better to see her feeling worse. But it was no good. In spite of my anger, her misery saddened me. Could an adult hurt like a child? Sometimes life was just too confusing.

I supposed it wasn't much of a trade for her, leaving Daniel in the grave, and taking me with her to America. Still, it wasn't much of a trade for me either, getting Sannah in place of my mother. No good at all.

Hannah's stepfather called out and relieved the awkward moment. "Come, *Montzleut*—come men—we must fix this wagon, and quickly." With that, he began unhitching the horses to let them graze on the steppe grass by the roadside. The other men rushed to assist, while Sahra helped Sannah straighten her skirts.

The problem was a broken reach, the long pole under the wagon that fastened the back wheels and axle to the front wheels and axle. It had been our bad luck to hit a big rock and a rut at the same moment. The front axle suddenly twisted, snapping the reach pole in half. With the reach gone, the back axle, wheels and all, had bounced out from under the wagon.

Tobias apologized over and over for hitting the rock. Digging through his toolbox, he pulled out wire, nails, pliers, a hammer, and an ax. Wagon breakdowns were common, and drivers traveled prepared.

As soon as the men had the wheels and the wagon box lined up, Andreas called me. "Now Paul, you must push the wheels under the wagon while we lift it up. The women will help, but remember, you are the man on this job and must take the lead." I thought I saw him wink to Jacob, but it didn't matter. His words were like goose grease to my pride.

"On three then," Jacob called, and he counted. "*Ansz, zwa, dreia!*" The men lifted together, and up went the back of the wagon. The women and I pushed the wheels, rolling them underneath. As I worked, I began to feel better, though my blistered hind end still stung as I bent to the task.

Soon the reach was splinted, nailed, and wired together. We had the wagon reloaded and the horses hitched by the time Tobias twisted the last strand of wire. We had lost only two hours, but if we were to catch the four o'clock train, the horses would have to trot.

Tobias cracked a driving whip in the air and we were off.

"This time," Andreas called, "I'll help you watch for rocks and ruts." He slapped Tobias playfully on the back. Nothing put a Hutterite man in a good mood like hard work that turned out right.

Chapter 17
The Train

The horses were blowing hard by the time we entered Alexandrovsk. At ten past four we came clipping down the street toward the rail station, past the Russian townsfolk in their high boots and baggy pants. They gawked as if we were the main show at the annual agricultural fair. Some pointed and laughed. We must have looked funny with our baggage thrown helter-skelter on the wagon and all of us perched on top, covered with dust. We leaned toward the station like contestants in a wagon race.

"I think I see smoke from the locomotive!" Jacob called.

"Yes, I see it too!" Sahra cried. "The train is still there."

"They must be building up the fire. Hurry, Tobias," Andreas urged.

Tobias gave rein and snapped the whip. The tired horses broke into a gallop.

Checkela leaped about on the baggage like a circus clown doing acrobatics. His father caught him by the arm and snapped, "Sit down before you bounce right out on your head!"

Clattering to the station platform, we could see the black locomotive steaming and hissing like a huge and powerful storybook beast. Black smoke from the coal fire in its belly billowed from the stack.

Michael Waldner, the colony preacher, stood beside the

train. He was yelling to a man in the locomotive. The man waved his arms angrily, and blew the whistle. We heard a rush of steam, and the big drive-wheels began to turn. It was leaving without us!

At that moment preacher Michael saw us. Leaping onto the locomotive ladder, he waved his hat and yelled at the engineer. The train stopped, and we heard a cheer from one of the train cars—the Sheromet people.

"Thank the Lord you made it, and just in time," the preacher said, rushing over to our wagon. "And the children are safe. Praise be! But hurry now, with your bags. The engineer thinks he has a schedule to keep."

Until that day, Friday, June 7, 1874, I thought horses were a fast way to travel. But that train could go over thirty miles an hour and do it all day without getting tired. We fairly sailed over the steppe.

I soon wished I could have ridden in the baggage car. It would have been more comfortable. The railway was not ready for so large a group, and we were a hundred and nine people jammed into a car made for sixty. Many of us had to stand—not that I wanted to sit anyway.

What a stew of sweat and emotion we were in! Some people were happy that Hannah and I were safe; others were angry that we had been late. Everyone was relieved that the trip was underway, excited over what lay ahead, and miserable over leaving familiar hearth and home. Children's shouts and women's tears mingled in the heat. There was the smell of coal smoke and the clickety-clack sound of steel wheels on the tracks.

In the middle of it all, with my face jammed between the shoulder blades of Fat Hans the shoemaker, I decided that if living with these people had been bad, traveling with them was worse. And that was when I made my decision.

• • •

"But what will you *do*?" Hannah asked. The worry in her voice gave me a small rush of pleasure. It also scared me. I hadn't actually thought ahead to what I would do.

"I don't really care," I replied. "I'll find something. Maybe work on a farm. The main thing is, I'll be on my own."

It was the first chance we'd had to talk since leaving. It was Sunday afternoon, and we had been sitting around the station in a city called Orel since eleven o'clock the night before. We had left the Russian Ukraine behind, and were in the Russian motherland—stuck. The Russians had lost our baggage car.

"So when?" Hannah asked.

"I'm not sure, but I will know when the right chance comes." I hadn't figured that out either, but it would have to be sometime when I could sneak my suitcase out of the baggage car. Then I'd hide when the train pulled out and be on my way—to somewhere. "In the meantime," I continued, "I'll just keep my arms tucked away from the buran wind."

"What?"

"Oh, never mind. It's something Andreas told me about a windmill." I was thinking of Sannah Basel.

"You're odd."

I took that as a compliment. I enjoyed the opportunity to impress Hannah. "I'll probably work somewhere for a couple of years, and then maybe go back to Hutterdorf." I was making my plans as I talked. "I figure on getting off in Berlin or maybe Hamburg. The Germans might be good to work for."

Hannah sighed. "Well I have to say, I think you're stupid."

My jaw dropped in disappointment. "How can you say that?"

"No one to live with, no more school, and no more church. You'll lose all the important things and you're only twelve. I think that's stupid."

"Typical girl," I replied. "You worry too much. I know what I'm doing."

"Typical boy!" she shot back. "No brain to think with. Do you still have your money at least? You'll need it."

I reached into my pocket, fingering the bills. "Right here," I said. "There's plenty to give me a good start. I wish that baggage car would get back, though. I need to hide the money in my suitcase before Sannah decides to wash my clothes." Everyone was getting grubby—especially me. Pants soaked with goose grease collect a lot of dirt.

"Well, at least with the baggage car gone you're safe."

"Why?"

"Nothing to change into. She'll be wanting you to change into your Sunday clothes for traveling. She won't take these and leave you naked."

"With Sannah Basel I wouldn't be too sure," I grumbled.

Hannah burst out laughing, her musical voice chiming like a song in our empty corner of the station yard. We had a spot to ourselves. Elsewhere, people were milling about, visiting or snoozing in the sun. I felt my ears getting hot. I had a feeling I wouldn't like what she was laughing at.

"What's so funny?" I challenged.

"You."

"Why? Was I telling jokes?"

"I just imagined you dancing around the station in your birthday suit while your Sannah Basel washed your clothes in the horse trough."

"Very funny. Hah, hah," I said sarcastically. The thought of running naked around the crowded station was enough to give me the shivers—even if it was a hot afternoon. "Didn't your mother teach you not to think rude thoughts?"

"Okay. I'm sorry." She paused, and then burst out giggling again. "With your money stuffed in your mouth."

I gave her my nastiest glare, though I had to admit it was

kind of funny, if you looked at it right. I felt my lips twitch.

"Really, I don't mean anything by it, but wouldn't that shock the *olten Ankelen*—the old grandmothers—to see you hopping around like a skinny grasshopper with a mouthful of money!"

Now that was too much. "*Wiry*, not skinny," I said indignantly.

"Wiriest little grasshopper in Russia."

I grabbed a handful of grass. "Here, Hannah—a grasshopper's favorite food. Let's see how you like it." I jumped at her, pretending to stuff it into her mouth. She laughed quietly, grabbing my wrists. I'd have wrestled her down, just for fun, except that if Graybeard noticed—or worse yet, Sannah, there would be trouble for sure. Wrestling with a girl was not proper at all.

That was when it hit me, like a punch in the gut. I would miss Hannah when I left. But why was she so interested in me? She thought we had something in common. Dead fathers. But if she knew what I knew about that night in the storm, she would see it was altogether different.

Chapter 18

Vanya the Great

The five juggling batons spun through the air like the whirling blades of a windmill. Always the windmill. I remembered Andreas' story. This was the playful wind for sure. I could feel it lifting my spirits.

At seven that morning, when we had pulled into the Vilna station in Russian Belarus, this man was there on the platform, already performing his juggling acts. The Russian's loose-fitting Cossack shirt flowed and rippled with the movements of his arms.

To avoid Sannah's attention, I had jumped quickly from the train and watched from off to one side. The juggler called to the weary travelers as they emerged, fixing first one and then another with his forceful gaze. His eyes were piercing and black, his straight nose jutting down between them. He was fascinating, and would have looked completely fierce, except for the softness of his mouth under his bushy, dangling mustache. He was old—at least forty or fifty.

A Cossack fur hat sat by his feet, and I watched in amazement as some Russians and Prussian Germans who had gathered to watch threw coins into it. He was making money by juggling!

But for all his amazing skill with batons and colored balls, he made no money from our group. The Hutterite mothers hurried their children past, and the elders spoke sharply to the young people who got too close. Circus people had a bad reputation, and their shows were considered entertainments of the devil. Even my own parents would not have approved. But I could hardly keep my eyes away.

The problem of how to survive when I ran away had bothered me for three days since my talk with Hannah. After all, I knew my five hundred rubles would not last forever. Maybe this was the answer. *If I could only learn to juggle!*

I fingered my money, then slipped it out of my pocket and counted it again. The wrinkled paper felt reassuring on my fingertips. I sighed with relief to find that it was still all there. Then, glancing up, I caught my breath. Had the juggler been watching? Had I seen his dark eyes on me just for a moment as he dropped the colored balls into his sack? I slipped the money back into my pocket.

Then he was juggling again. Knives this time! It was a mystery how he flipped them through the air so fast and caught them by the handles. If I could only do that!

A hand grabbed my arm, and I nearly jumped out of my shoes. "Paul, look," said a voice.

I did. Right into those luminous brown eyes again. "Hannah, what are you trying to do—scare the liver out of me?"

"Only if it's *Hohna Leber*—chicken liver. I just wondered if you noticed anything over there." She pointed to the baggage car. A couple of the women were getting a rail worker to open the doors. Until now, there had been no chance to get at the baggage since the Russians found the car and re-hooked it to our train. "It's your chance to hide your money."

We slipped out of sight on the far side of the train, where no one would see us.

"As soon as the women leave, we can go in," Hannah said.

However, seeing the open door, more people flocked to the car. One of them was Sannah, who soon left, carrying my Sunday clothes under her arm. We waited at the edge of a field, shielded by train cars and a clump of bushes.

That was when the juggler came. "What are you doing out here, *Rebyata*—children?" he asked in Russian.

For the second time in five minutes, Hannah clutched my arm, this time out of fear. "If he tries anything, just scream," I whispered. "Practically everyone is close enough to hear."

"What do you want?" I asked him.

"I often rest in the fields after performing," he said smoothly. "I noticed you watching me. Do you like juggling?" His voice was softer and friendlier than his looks would suggest. I began to relax.

"To be honest," I said, "I thought it was wonderful."

He chuckled. "I like your opinion, boy. But I think most of your people would disagree. A man could starve performing for them."

"If you really were starving," Hannah spoke up, "we would take you in and feed you. But we are not allowed that kind of entertainment."

"Ah, so the *golubka*—the little pigeon—speaks too. Tell me, golubka, where are you traveling?"

"America," she replied tersely.

He leered at Hannah and touched her cheek with a dirty finger. "How lucky you are, golubka. America is a good place for one so lovely to seek her fortune."

Hannah gripped my arm tighter. "We have to go," she said, trying to pull me away. I stayed where I was. "You go ahead."

"Your little girlfriend is afraid of me," the man smiled.

"She is not my girlfriend," I said, wondering if he was dangerous.

"And not afraid," Hannah added. "We have to go. That's all."

"As you wish," the Russian said, with a courtly nod of his head. "I wish you a pleasant day." He turned, as if to go.

Would anyone with mischief in mind leave us that easily? I wondered.

"Wait!" I cried. He turned. "I was wondering . . ." I stammered.

"Yes?"

"I was wondering if you could teach me to juggle."

He set his sack down and eyed me up and down, as if deciding whether I was worth his time. Then he broke into a grin. "Why not? Vanya the Great is always willing to help someone who is eager to learn. What is your name?"

"Paul," I said, holding out my hand. "My name is Paul."

Hannah's grip tightened even more on my arm. She spoke in German, so the Russian would not understand. "*Dei Nomen ist Anfoltich*—your name is Stupid—but if you stay, I'm staying with you."

Chapter 19

The Thief

Juggling is easier—and harder—than it looks. Within five minutes, Vanya the Great had me juggling three soft leather balls filled with wheat. Well, sort of juggling.

"The trick," he said, "is to keep looking up at the balls. Do not follow them to your hands or the others will get away before you look back. Watch them in the air, and your hands will know on their own where to make the catch."

After a few tries, I could catch three in a row. But every time I started thinking I could keep them going, I missed, and the whole thing would fly apart. I'd be snatching at air while the balls landed by my feet.

"*Nyet, nyet*—no, no," Vanya laughed. "You are throwing them too soon." He stepped behind me and reached his arms around to take my wrists, bobbing them up and down in a smooth rhythm. I sniffed. He smelled like *samogon*—the liquor some of the Russian peasants who had worked for my father drank.

"Do not be in such a hurry to throw the balls," he coached. "There is plenty of time. Yes?"

"If you say so." I tried again, this time doing five throws before they fell.

"There, you see? You are better already."

Before long, I could do seven throws, and then ten.

"Ha ha, your friend is a natural, is he not?" Vanya said to

Hannah, slapping me on the back.

"What would I know about it?" Hannah replied sourly.

Vanya pulled a pouch labeled *Troika* from his sack. It was tobacco. He rolled a cigarette. "Take it from me," he replied. "This fellow could soon be good enough to juggle for the Tsar. Were I looking for a partner, he would be the man." He laughed. "Vanya and Vanka—how's that for a team?"

I frowned. *Vanka* was Russian for "little rascal." Could Vanya and the Little Rascal really be a juggling act? Or was he only teasing?

Vanya laughed again, and held the tobacco can my way. "*Pappeross*—cigarette?"

I shook my head. Cigarettes stank. But the aroma of hope filled my mind as an idea took shape. Maybe this was my chance.

"So, Paul, why are you interested in learning to juggle?" Vanya asked. "Is it to defy your parents, or maybe the rules of your own church? Is that it? Is the little rascal also a rebel?"

"They are not my parents," I replied simply.

He raised his eyebrows. "An orphan, then?"

"Not exactly," Hannah interrupted. "He has an uncle and an aunt who—"

"An aunt who hates me, and these are not my people," I broke in. This was my chance to tell him everything and get him to take me away. Like steam from a locomotive, my story rushed out—about my parents being killed, how I did not fit in, how Sannah had destroyed the only things left from my mother, and how I had made up my mind to run away.

When I finished, Vanya was staring at me strangely, his dark eyes squinting as if the smoke from his cigarette was stinging them. It reminded me of how my father had looked when he had to butcher old *Butterkuchel*, our favorite sow. It hurt, but we had to have food.

"What are you looking at?" I asked nervously.

He gave a kind of sad, half grin. "Nothing, boy. Maybe you remind me of someone I used to know."

"Somebody you liked?"

"Ha! You could say that," he chuckled. "Yes, somebody I liked. Now, enough of your questions. Why are you telling me about these troubles of yours?"

"Well, I was thinking . . ." I didn't know how to say it, so I just blurted it out. "I was thinking maybe you *do* need a partner. I was thinking you could take me with you. I . . . I could practice all the time, and be good enough to juggle for the Tsar. Vanya and Vanka, like you said."

For the third time that day, Hannah grabbed my arm. "No, Paul," she said, going back to German. *"Du kennst ihn nit—* you don't even know him. He could be *ein Mörder—*a murderer—or anything."

"Hannah, *du vorstehts gor nit—*you don't understand. This is my perfect chance."

Vanya the Great cleared his throat. All of a sudden, he looked tired. "Listen boy," he began, "when I spoke of a partner, I did not know you wanted to run away. I cannot take you."

"But—"

"Do you think I need police hunting me down for kidnapping?" he snapped.

"But it's not kidnapping. I *want* to go."

"Ayi, tell that to the police with your bearded elders reporting your disappearance." He waved his hand as if to end the conversation. "Besides, Vanya works alone. It is hard enough to feed one hungry belly without an extra mouth swallowing the food."

I had the perfect answer. "If that is the problem, I can buy food for us both," I offered, going for my pocket.

"I don't think you should trust him," Hannah cautioned, in German again.

"I have made up my mind." My fingers reached down into my pocket—and down, right to the bottom. *Nothing!* The money was gone! I tried again, frantically jerking my hand back and forth and around in my pocket. But it was no good. There was nothing in it.

"What is the matter, boy?" Vanya asked. "You look as if you are fighting a snake in that pocket."

"My money!" I cried. "It's gone—all gone. It's all I had left." I ran back and forth, looking on the ground where I had been juggling. Nothing.

Stunned, I flopped to the ground. "Mueter and Fater," I muttered in a daze. "My treasure box, and now my money. What am I going to do?" I wanted to cry. I looked at Vanya, as if he might have an answer. "I had it only an hour ago. I checked it when—" I looked into his eyes. And then I knew. And my anger saved me from crying.

"Pickpocket!" I spat. "There was a snake in my pocket all right! You stole my money!"

"Boy, what are you talking about?"

"No wonder you don't like the police. I'll call the station-master and make you give it back. They'll arrest you for a thief."

"Boy, you don't know what you're talking about," Vanya said casually. He shrugged. "In my opinion, you never had a pocketful of money. But if you did, it is also my opinion that the aunt you dislike so much knew nothing about it. She would never have let you keep it. So you may want to call the stationmaster, but who will believe you when you say some-thing was stolen that even your aunt knew nothing about?"

As soon as he said it, I knew he was right. Hannah and I were the only ones who knew about the money. If I said this man had stolen five hundred rubles from me, everyone would think I was the biggest liar in Russia—a liar who was turning Hannah bad right along with me.

"I thought you were somebody special," I said dejectedly. "Vanya the Great! What a *dorak*—fool—I was to admire you."

Then I sat there, expecting Vanya to walk off with my money. There was not a thing I could do about it. But he just stood there with that squinty look in his eyes, as if he were looking way off, somewhere else.

I wondered what was wrong with Hannah. She was moving her lips and mumbling under her breath like she was talking the whole thing out with herself. Being around such rough people was probably too much for a girl to handle. I wanted to kick myself for not listening to her. I shouldn't have had anything to do with this man. Now my money was gone, and Hannah was scared out of her wits. And it was all my fault.

Suddenly Vanya kicked at a rock. It thunked on his boot and skittered between Hannah and me. "Ah, *Nye mogu*—I cannot," he muttered angrily. Quick as a cat, he leaned over me and tugged on my ear.

"Ouch! Stop it," I cried.

"What's in there, boy?" he said. "You should keep your ears cleaned out better. See what I have found?" He drew back his hand. I gasped. It was full of Russian rubles! Then he flicked my other ear with his other hand and another fistful of rubles appeared.

Chapter 20

A Change of Heart

Vanya the Great fanned the money with his thumb. I stared, openmouthed, as he counted it in front of me. All five hundred rubles were there!

"Come now, boy, push your eyeballs back into your head," he said, tucking the bills in my hand. "A bird might mistake them for grapes, and pluck them out."

"You . . . you gave it back," I stammered, dumbfounded.

"I never had it," he said firmly. "I found it in your ears. Now aren't you sorry for accusing me?"

He had taken it, of course. He knew it. I knew it. And he knew that I knew it. Still, if he wanted to pretend, that was fine with me, as long as I had the money.

"I . . . uh, okay, I'm sorry," I muttered.

Hannah was looking up at the clouds. She did not seem afraid anymore.

"So, boy," he said, "as you can see, we are not meant to be partners." The sadness was back in his eyes. I wondered what this strange man was thinking. Fifteen minutes ago, I had thought he was a hero. Two minutes ago, I had thought he was evil. Now he seemed all mixed up somewhere in between. Was nothing in life simple?

"You are a strong-headed young man," Vanya sighed. "I said you reminded me of someone. It was myself. Vanya knows what it is for a boy to have no parents."

I studied him. Was that why he had returned the money?

"Tell me," Vanya said, "What will you do now?"

It was a hard question, especially in my state of confusion. "Go back to my old plan, I guess. I was going to work on a farm in Germany. Or maybe I can still try juggling, if I learn it better." I didn't sound convincing.

"In that case, I have to tell you, you will make no money juggling three balls. You need to do four or five, or even seven. I myself can juggle seven, when my nerves are good."

His nerves must have needed calming just then, because he dug into his sack and pulled out a worn metal flask. He opened the lid and took a drink. I could smell the samogon again. He screwed on the lid with a flourish, and flipped it spinning over his shoulder so it landed in the sack. "And you have to have style," he said with a flashy, fake grin.

Then the smile disappeared. "Never look for comfort in the bottle," he said seriously. "It becomes a fishhook you cannot get out of your skin."

"I'm sorry if you have a problem," I replied, feeling embarrassed.

"Ha!" Vanya laughed, slapping his leg. "You are so young, with so much to learn. Let me give you some good advice. Go to America. They say America is a place for new beginnings. And I think you are one who needs a new beginning. Can you bring your parents back by staying here? You must go ahead in life. Do not stay where everything is old, old like me, and falling apart," he said with a halfway grin.

"And something else. I wish you would believe me when I tell you the family you have is better than no family at all. Go with these people to America. And who knows? If you still have to run away, maybe by the time you get there you will be good enough to earn money as a juggler."

"*Golubka*," he said, catching Hannah's eye, "you are a smart girl. I think your angry young friend could benefit from your wisdom. He was foolish to trust me. But one thing." He switched to German. "I am not yet bad enough to be *ein Mörder*—a murderer." He laughed. "A traveling entertainer must speak many languages to survive. Though I must say this Hutterite German of yours sounds odd to me."

Hannah's mouth fell open in surprise, and my eyes bugged out. He had understood every word of Hannah's warnings to me, but had not let on.

Recovering her composure, Hannah met his gaze. "No," she said. "I do not think you are so bad as that. And anyway, even if you were, there is one thing that doesn't change. *Isus ljubit tebya,*" she said in Russian—"Jesus loves you."

He laughed again. "If he does, he loves a *dorak*—an idiot. Five hundred rubles—*ayi yi,* what a dorak." He flicked my ear with a finger. "You look after that money. There are many who would be happy to take it from you." Then he turned, with his sack slung heavily over his shoulder, and walked back to the station.

"Why did you tell him that?" I asked, watching Vanya disappear around the front of the train.

"Because it's true, Paul. No matter what you think you have done, Jesus never quits loving you. Sometimes we need to be reminded of that."

Hannah had that look again, with the light in her eyes that shone right into you, and I knew she was not talking about the Russian. She was on my case again.

There was a loud bang as two railcars bumped into one another. "Hey, look," I said, glad of a distraction, "they're shunting the cars." The Russians were always switching the cars around. I had lost track of how many times we'd had to change coaches. At least they had added an extra after the first day so we could all sit down.

"Let's go, before they close up the baggage car," I said.

We ran to the car. The open door was on the opposite side,

toward the station. I looked underneath. "Come on," I said. "We'll go under. I think they're all gone."

"What if it runs over us?" Hannah asked.

"It can't."

"Why not?"

"It's not even hooked up," I explained, pointing to where the locomotive was moving another car. "You're a genius for machines, aren't you?" I teased. "No wonder women have to stick to sewing."

"Is that so?" Hannah challenged. "Don't you know that men used to be in charge of sewing?"

"Oh sure. When?"

"In the Garden of Eden. That's why Adam and Eve had nothing to wear."

"Very funny. I just died laughing," I replied. "Come on."

I took her hand and we crawled under the car. The train wheels looked awfully big as we crawled on our bellies right in front of them, but we were soon through. It took a bit of sorting to find my little leather suitcase. There wasn't much in it, but I felt fortunate to have been allowed my own bag, instead of sharing Andreas and Sannah's big trunk. I shook everything out. A thick, leather pad was sewn into the bottom of the bag, for sturdiness. It was easy to cut a few threads with my knife and slip the money underneath the pad. I stuffed my things back in, and buckled it shut.

"Now maybe it will be safe," I sighed. "I never knew looking after money could be such a worry."

"*Joh*, just think of how much worry Vanya the Great almost relieved you of today."

"I know. Strange that he had such a change of heart," I said.

"I guess you could say that," Hannah agreed.

"So, did you expect him to pull a juggling knife out of his bag and kill us? I don't remember seeing you that scared before."

"Scared?" Hannah asked with surprise.

"Well, *joh*, you were mumbling away like you had lost your mind. What were you jabbering about anyway?"

"About a change of heart for your juggler. I was praying."

"Praying?"

"Yes, Paul, praying," she said sarcastically. "I think you may have heard of it in church."

"You mean you think—?"

"Why not, Paul? Sometimes God changes hearts. Right?"

"If you say so."

"Why don't you let him change your heart too, Paul? I think you're mad at God for the things that have happened."

Am I mad at God, or is God mad at me? I wondered. "Lay off, Hannah. You don't know anything about it."

Just then the train whistle blew, and we heard the familiar huffing of the locomotive as it gathered power to leave the station. But our baggage car was not moving! I stuck my head out the door, and my heart leaped into my mouth. "The train is leaving without us!" I shouted back to Hannah.

Chapter 21

Chasing the Train

"What do you mean the train's leaving?" Hannah shouted. "It can't be! We're still here!"

"I know we're still here! But the train is going." The next thing I knew, Hannah was leaping out of the baggage car, running before she hit the ground. "Come on!" she yelled. "We can still catch it."

Luckily, steam trains do not gain speed quickly. We pounded along the station platform after the end car. Vanya the Great was bending over to put his juggling balls and batons away. Going by, we nearly bowled him over.

His shout of surprise and raspy laugh faded as I sprinted away. Everything was a blur: my feet pounding the platform boards, Hannah's skirts flying ahead, and the train rocking alongside. It was crazy to be so desperately trying to catch the train, after I had looked for a chance to get away! *To catch the train*. I'd have laughed if I'd had enough breath. First in a broken wagon, now on foot—catching the train was getting harder all the time.

I caught up to Hannah just as she grabbed the handrail, but I couldn't jump until she got on. Her skirts were giving her trouble, tying up her legs. *Hurry Hannah*! I thought. I had no extra breath for shouting. The train was picking up speed, and I started to lose ground. The platform ended, and now, instead of running on smooth boards, I was scrambling over dirt. It was uneven and loose. I stumbled, but somehow caught my balance.

I had often heard that desperation gives a person extra power, and as the train pulled away, I felt a surging rush of energy. There was power in my chest, and my feet hardly seemed to touch the ground.

Hannah had at last crawled up to the second step. I strained forward, reaching for the rail. The train was going too fast for me now, but I made a desperate lunge and felt my fingers wrap around the steel handhold. The train pulled me along, and I bounded beside it like a great, leaping frog.

Finally I got hold with my other hand, and with one last jump, swung a leg up onto the stairs. But I was stuck—halfway on, with one leg dangling down. I imagined the leg swinging too far under the train and getting ripped off by one of those big steel wheels. I struggled harder. Then my hat was gone.

"Hannah, give me a hand," I croaked. The next thing I knew, she had me by the hair, yanking for all she was worth. Then she grabbed a pant leg, and I was on.

I looked down. The ground was zipping by as the train neared its running speed.

"Thanks," I panted. "That was close."

"It was a pleasure," she replied with a wild-looking grin. Her face was flushed with excitement, and for a moment I couldn't help noticing how beautiful she was.

"*Joh*, I bet it was a pleasure," I replied. "You nearly tore my scalp off."

"Well, sorry, but it was the handiest part of you to grab."

We sat on an outside step, out of sight of the rest of the passengers. For a while we did not move, as we caught our breath. I figured we were going to catch a lot more than our breath at any moment from elders and parents, but no one came out.

It was still only nine o'clock in the morning, and the shadow of the train raced beside us on the ground. Unlike Hannah and me, it had no trouble keeping up. The wind was relaxing and cool, blowing through my hair. I thought of my bare head. A Hutterite was always to wear a hat outside. It was just what I needed—to lose my hat. *More ammunition for Sannah.*

When we finally entered the car, we were greeted by the sound of howling. More little ones were fighting or getting spanked. Sometimes it seemed there were just too many little children in a Hutterite group, either getting cranky or sick. I was glad I didn't have to look after them.

Seeing us enter, Sahra cried in surprise, "Hannah, *Lieba*—love—what are you doing here? I thought you were in the other car with Paul's family."

That was good news. Sannah was in the other car.

It wasn't surprising that Sahra hadn't known where we were. The train switched cars so frequently, it was hard to keep track of who was where. Graybeard had given up on keeping Hannah away from me, though I didn't know why. Maybe Sahra had spoken with him. She, at least, always treated me politely.

I looked around. Hardly anyone paid attention to us. As amazing as it seemed, nobody had noticed how we came aboard.

Hannah answered her mother. "No, Mueter, we were not in the other car."

Of course not, I thought. On Russian trains, there are no doors between cars. I hoped she would not explain to her mother what had happened. Hannah liked to be truthful.

"We just came in from the steps out there."

Well, that's true, I mused. *Even if she forgot to mention how we got there.*

"While the train was moving you stood out there!" Sahra cried. "Hannah! You might have fallen off and been killed or left behind."

How true, how true, I silently agreed.

"Yes, Mueter, that is exactly what we were afraid of. We won't be doing that again."

"Be sure you do not, Hannah." Then she stared at me. "And, Paul, where is your *Katus*—your hat? You know you should wear it."

Before I could open my mouth, Hannah spoke for me. "The wind blew it off the train, Mueter."

"There, you see how dangerous it is. It might have been one of *you* falling off instead of a hat. Oh, I will be glad to get off these trains."

I hoped with all my heart that Hannah's mother would never learn the rest of the story. I didn't know which would shock her worse—knowing Hannah had almost been left behind, or that she had prevented it with a dangerous leap onto a moving train.

Chapter 22
Through Germany

By eight that evening, we reached the end of Russia at the border town of Wierzbolo. The mean and greedy border guards lined us up like prisoners. They counted and recounted us, then made each person pay six rubles and ninety-six kopecks just to leave the country. Then we waited. And waited. Finally, we got to cross the border. We had reached Prussia, of the mighty German Empire.

Then we had to wait some more—for our baggage car, this time because of a broken coupler.

We spent the night in a park, which was when Sannah finally brought me my change of clothes—and found out about my hat! With the sun setting behind her, she puffed and steamed like a locomotive. Hannah's mother was close by and eventually said in her quiet way, "Sannah, perhaps one should give thanks that it was only a Katus. There is so much more to love in a young man than in a hat."

Sannah stopped cold. Her jaw worked a couple of times like it didn't know how to quit. Then she started blinking and the strangest thing happened. She stared at me, surprised and confused, as if she had never seen me before. It was like Fater once looked when the scrawny hen he had decided to kill suddenly started laying beautiful, big eggs.

Then Sannah walked off and sat by herself. For a second I thought she might cry. A ridiculous idea. She probably felt foolish for letting Sahra ruin her tirade.

It was a long cold night, since our blankets were still in the missing baggage car, but the next day was sunny. We gathered for outdoor worship, thanking God for a safe journey so far, and asking him to bless the rest of our travels.

When our baggage finally arrived, we headed into Prussia. In six days, we had come a little over halfway to Hamburg on the Russian trains. The efficient German railway would do the second half in only two.

"So what have you decided?" asked Hannah, later in the day.

I knew what she meant. "America," I said simply. "I'm going."

Hannah said nothing. I watched her face. Not even a smile. Then a small flash in her eyes, just enough so I knew she was pleased. Not that I really cared, I told myself.

• • •

Berlin was amazing. Not even the adults had seen anything like the railway station there. Thousands of people crowded and bustled everywhere, going in all directions at once.

The train let out a huge, hissing breath of steam and relaxed at the platform. Hannah sat beside me, peering out the window. "I didn't know there were so many people in the world," she said.

"Or trains," I added, over the sound of steam whistles and squealing brakes. The place was a web of platforms, tracks, and locomotives. "Where do they all travel, I wonder?"

Preacher Michael shouted, "Brethren and sisters! We must switch to another train. Stay together and pray to God we do not lose any of our children among this godless rabble."

We stepped into a din of train sounds, shouting, and music. Smells of sweat, coal smoke, and food mingled together. The aromas were sickening and tempting by turns as one drifted into another.

Porters offered to carry bags for money. Men offered overnight rooms for money. Musicians played harmonicas or violins or accordions for money. Jugglers entertained for money. I'd often heard the phrase, "Money makes the world go around." Now I understood. This place was spinning.

The women fretted over their small children as we pushed through the smoke, steam, and confusion. Elders muttered Bible verses about how crowded and wide is the road to destruction.

To me it was exciting, but scary. Hutterites had lived on the quiet steppe land for so long that the moon would not have seemed stranger than this station.

"Look at that juggler," Hannah said as we bustled along with the crowd. "He makes Vanya the Great look like Vanya the Has-Been."

She was right. This juggler looked fresh and young, with fancy new clothes and flashy batons. He chattered cheerily to the people gathered round as he juggled through his legs and behind his back, his hands a blur of speed. I wondered how anyone could be so fast.

"I'm glad you decided on America," Hannah said, so only I could hear.

Looking around, I was glad too. Where would a runaway go in a crazy mix-up like this? I remembered Vanya's advice: staying behind could not change what had happened. Maybe a new start in a new land would be better.

Then again, maybe I was just chickenhearted.

"Don't forget," I said, as much to myself as to Hannah, "I'll be leaving when we get to America."

• • •

Hamburg was every bit as busy as Berlin. We arrived there at nine o'clock in the evening. Once again, hustlers were everywhere. We wandered the station aimlessly until an agent finally led us to the emigration building—a place where people could stay while waiting for their ship to leave. It was a huge structure, five stories high.

Walking beside me, Andreas pointed to the back of the building. "Look Paul, the wall is over the water."

Peering through the dim light, I could see giant pillars sticking straight out of the river, holding the building up. "If you jumped out a window, you would land right in the river," I said.

"Handy for a bath, don't you think?" Andreas chuckled. One thing about Andreas, he tried to be friendly. If Sannah were more like him, things might not be so bad.

We went through the front door and entered a great hall. Fiddle music swirled through the room, and men and women danced across the floor, laughing joyously.

"Look away, people," Preacher Michael called to us, "lest temptation lead you astray." But who could help looking at the fun? I gaped until my eyes bulged. It was easy to see why Hutterites built colonies far away from cities. People couldn't be tempted by what they didn't know.

Two days later, more than a hundred Hutterites from Hutterdorf arrived on a train to join us. Some were communal people, led by Preacher Darius Walter, and some were noncommunal. We would travel the rest of the way together. The elders bought tickets to sail on a ship called the *Hammonia*. It belonged to Hamburg American, one of the two biggest steamship companies in Germany.

Only two days after the Darius Walter group arrived, we were counted like sheep and herded onto a steamboat ferry. Our ship was anchored somewhere out on the Elbe River. Hamburg was almost fifty miles from the sea, but the Elbe was so big that oceangoing ships could sail all the way to the city. It took us two hours to get to the *Hammonia*.

I heard one of the younger women say in a worried voice to Sannah Basel, "Ah, the ocean must be powerful big if it takes so long just to get to the ship."

"Don't worry," Sannah replied, "the Lord will go with us."

And then I saw it. I couldn't have imagined a bigger, more amazing boat. Three hundred and thirty feet long, it was like a massive island in the river. Our ferryboat was like a little piece of cork, bobbing in the water beside it. I looked straight up the side of a towering iron wall. I could hardly wait to climb on board.

Chapter 23
The *Hammonia*

The deep-throated steam whistle of the *Hammonia* bellowed good-bye to the disappearing land. We had sailed out the mouth of the Elbe River and down the coast. Now we were leaving LeHavre, France, the last port until the American city of New York. There was nothing but ocean before us, and the first twelve years of my life sank slowly into the misty sea in our wake.

I thought of the past, and all of the love we were leaving behind. For me: Mueter and Fater. For Hannah: her father. For Sannah: her son Daniel. How many others were leaving the ghosts of past joy in Russia? Many tears fell as the ship pulled away. But, like it or not, we were on to a new beginning. There was no stopping now. "Good-bye," I whispered. "Forgive me, Mueter—I should never have wanted to leave."

• • •

On our second day out, everyone was crowded onto the flat wooden deck, enjoying the sun and the sea. A slight breeze puffed the sails. Up on the forecastle—the raised deck over the crew's quarters at the front of the ship—Sahra held her baby. Hannah watched four-year-old Maria, and Checkela romped like a rabbit with the other boys his age. *Somebody ought to tie him up*, I thought, *before he jumps right into the sea.*

I stood at the prow, gazing ahead as the ship sliced through the clear, smooth water. The air smelled clean and salty.

"Just imagine," Hannah said dreamily, "The pointer is showing the way to America. I wonder what it will be like."

"It's the bowsprit, not a pointer," I said disdainfully. I had to admit, though, the big pole sticking out over the water at the front of the ship did look like a giant pointer. But I had been questioning the crew, so I knew better. "The bowsprit is where they tie the front sails."

The ship was fascinating. It had everything people needed for living. There were sleeping rooms, eating rooms, bathrooms, a sickroom, a kitchen, and big rooms with chairs for reading or visiting. And there were plenty of workplaces. Some sailors worked in the engine room, shoveling coal into the hot furnaces that made the steam. Some kept the giant steam engines thrusting properly to power the ship. Others set the sails to catch the wind for more power, while still others cleaned and painted to stop the rust. It reminded me of a floating Hutterite colony, with everyone living and working together for the good of all. Of course there were a couple of big differences. No sailors' wives and families lived on board —and sailing was an adventure.

"Wouldn't it be great to travel the world as a sailor?" I said to Hannah.

She gave an exasperated sigh. "At least as good as being a juggler, wouldn't you say? Why don't you stop thinking about getting away, and grab hold of the real dream in front of us? Just think! We're starting a new life in America. No worries about the army. No worries about trouble like the Jews get in Russia. Just freedom, to live our faith like God wants. Haven't you wondered if God has a purpose for you in that?"

I frowned. "I don't think God has a purpose for me," I said, irritably. "And anyway, if what happened to my parents was for a purpose, who wants it?"

As the sun sank low, a round silver moon shone faintly in the purple sky behind us. Ahead, a spectacular sunset lit up banks of towering clouds on the horizon. They were silver-edged and dark, with mixtures of bright orange and red swirling inside. Beneath the clouds the sky was a soft apricot, melting into a rosy sea. It was as if we were steaming right into an enormous picture painted on canvas. My skin prickled in the heavy air.

Everyone stared at the view. Even Checkela quit leaping about. I saw him sitting by himself in the middle of a heavy coil of rope. The rope was rolled up in a lidless box bolted to the deck. He seemed almost hypnotized, leaning back in his little nest.

"Storm coming," a sailor said, moving through our midst. "We'll need to go below soon." I looked aloft to the rigging. Sailors were clambering up and down like monkeys, lowering the sails.

As the sunset's glory faded, we cleared the deck. Adults with little children went first. Then the little boys, tired now, trooped down together. Hannah disappeared with little Maria. Even the young men were going below. I stepped out of sight behind the huge foremast that thrust through the forecastle deck. I wanted to be alone in the quiet. I was still not used to being crowded together with the communal Hutterites, especially on trains and this ship.

A brisk wind began to blow. I breathed deeply of the salty air, and thought about the strange events that had brought me here to the middle of the Atlantic Ocean. Everything had happened so quickly.

A short time ago I had wanted so badly to be here—my big dream of America. Well, that dream was shattered now. Instead of embracing the future, I seemed to be only running from the past. So much for dreams. A heaviness came over me, like the oppressive air that settled over the water.

I was lonely. Beneath the huge, dark sky, with the endless sea turning cold and gray, I was nothing but a small dot in the middle of nowhere. Hannah thought God had a purpose for everyone's life. Where was God's purpose in mine?

Anger welled up inside me. *"Why?"* I cried into the gathering wind. "Why did you listen to my prayer? Don't you know I didn't want them to die?"

Slumping to my knees, I shivered in the cooling air, feeling more alone than I had since I watched Mueter and Fater disappear into the depths of the ground. Darkening waters began to rise around the ship, and an equally dark idea entered my mind. Why not jump and end the whole thing—just close my eyes and sink into the great nothingness of the ocean? I shuddered at the thought of the cold, dark waters closing over me. *No!* If I was lonely now, the bottomless depths could only be worse. There had to be a better way— if only I could find it.

Storm coming, the sailor had said. The clouds were approaching quickly in the dimming light. The ship began to rock on the rising swell. Still, the day had been so calm I didn't see how it could be much of a storm.

And then, with a crash that nearly shook me off the deck, the first burst of thunder shattered the sky.

Chapter 24

Storm at Sea

I never knew a wind could whip the ocean into a rocking frenzy so fast. The heaving sea-swell rose and fell like the sides of a huge, panting animal, and wind roared in the rigging.

I watched, fascinated, for a moment, then climbed down the stairs from the forecastle to the main deck. Amidships, I clung to the rail and watched in amazement as a huge wave rolled in. I saw we were in the middle of a trough formed by two waves. The *Hammonia* was like an ant between furrows of earth at plowing time. How could such a huge ship suddenly seem so small? Flecks of foam spattered my face as wind blasted over the wave tops. Fear clutched my insides.

The ship tilted up at the front and rolled from side to side as we climbed the towering wall of water. As we hit the top, I looked out across the waves. There was nothing but more waves, like ripples on a huge gray washboard, as far as I could see. Facing the fury of the wind, I thought of the terrible steppe burans back home. But instead of whipping grass and dirt into a skin-ripping dust storm, this wind whipped rain and waves into a confusion of foam and spray.

The ship rushed down into the wave trough again, and my stomach rolled over. At the bottom, we straightened out once more before another wave crashed into the ship's side. Water surged over the rail and across the deck, knocking my feet from under me. If I had not been hanging on, I would have been swept away with the wave.

Now I was scared. Were waves supposed to get this high? Could a ship stay afloat in a sea like this? More thunder boomed as lightning flashed overhead, and a new fear gripped me. Could lightning hit the rail of a ship, like hitting the rail on a front yard fence?

A jagged sword of lightning stabbed wickedly into the sea, with a deafening roar of thunder. The thrashing rain and waves were a jumble of shapes beyond the ship. Did I see people in the crackle of blue light on the water? Mueter and Fater? Was I about to die like them? Was God going to strike me with the storm? Then as suddenly as it appeared, the lightning died, and the vision flew apart in a splash of water. My mind was playing tricks on me.

I ran, stumbling with the roll of the ship, toward the back of the main deck. Near the dividing rope was the open doorway leading down to the inside of the ship. On the other side of the rope was the first class area. The rich people had the back of the ship, including the high poop deck at the ship's end. It was abandoned now, but I remembered watching them in the afternoon, envying their fancy deck chairs and their umbrellas for keeping the sun off. Suddenly it seemed ridiculous. What difference would a fancy deck chair make if the ship went down in the storm?

I dashed into the shelter of the stairway just as the next wave hit. Water splashed around my ankles as I leaped onto the steps—into the arms of a sailor. I nearly knocked us both down the stairs.

"What?" he shouted in surprise. "*Bist du verrückt?*—are you crazy? Get down inside!"

"Is the ship going to sink?" I asked, ignoring his command.

"Of course not," he roared angrily. "The *Hammonia* can ride any storm in the Atlantic, but I should whip you to slivers

for being on deck in this weather. The decks are closed, don't
you know? Do you want to get washed into the deep?"

"I didn't mean to be out," I tried to explain. "I just—"

We heard a commotion at the bottom of the stairs. Someone
was crying and coming up the steps. It was a woman.

"What? Another one!" the sailor spat, dashing down the
long stairs to stop her.

"My Checkela!" the voice called. "I cannot find my
Checkela." It was Sahra. *What mischief has Checkela got
into now?* I wondered.

The sailor jerked his thumb up at me. "Is that him?" Sahra
met my eye. "No, no, not him. *Paul!*" she shouted. "Have
you seen Checkela?"

"No, I—"

"Get down, boy!" the sailor shouted angrily.

"My Checkela," Sahra wailed.

"He is not here, woman. Now get back. I am battening the
hatchway closed. Come down, boy!" he shouted.

"But my *son*. Help me find him. He could be—"

"He is probably hiding somewhere," said the sailor. "Probably sneaked into first class." The sailor hustled Sahra out of
sight into the corridor.

Another wave splashed over the hatchway. *Checkela! In
the box full of rope!* Before I could think, I was fighting my
way back across the deck toward the forecastle. *What if the
little boy had fallen asleep when everyone left? He would be
awake and terrified by now, if he hadn't already been . . .* The
thought was too terrible to finish.

The wind had risen into a howling gale, and the waves
were more terrifying than ever. They towered like mountains,
avalanches rolling toward the ship. It was impossible to tell
the rain from wind-whipped spray. I reached the mainmast
rigging before the next wave washed over the deck. Hugging
tightly to the ropes, I held on while the water rushed past,

clutching at my legs, trying to take me with it.

As soon as it passed, I scrambled on, past the big front funnel, slipping and falling as the ship galloped over the top of the wave. I crawled on my knees to a capstan—a drum with cable wrapped around it—by a dark deckhouse. I grabbed the cable as the most enormous wave yet reared over the ship. Frayed cable strands cut my hands as the water charged through the rail like a thrashing serpent from the deep. I held on in terror, recalling a picture I had once seen of a gigantic octopus reaching onto a ship and dragging a sailor into the sea. I heard the roar of water in my ears as it washed over my head. I had never been so afraid in my life. The raging power of the storm was all around, wet and cold, and roaring from the angry sky and the bottomless deep.

Choking on the water, my body stretched straight out with its force, I was sure I was about to drown. I tried to call out to God, but even in my fear my stubborn heart would not let me do it. Desperately, I clung to the sharp cable, the force of the water prying at my fingers. They were slipping. I knew I could not hold on much longer. The wave seemed to last forever.

I was about to die, an idiot washed overboard in a raging Atlantic storm. What was I doing out here? I remembered what Hannah had said when I threw myself at Vanya the Great. *Dei Nomen ist Anfoltich.* I *was* stupid, and about to drown.

Then, as the force of the water peaked, I felt my fear wash away like dirt from the deck of the ship. From somewhere out of the storm a strange peace came over me. Somehow I knew the sea would not get me. I had a job to do, and nothing was going to stop me. As the wave passed, I mustered up a new sense of courage and determination. Checkela needed my help.

I rose and dashed toward the forecastle. I felt the wind whip my hair, and realized I had lost another *Katus*, my second hat in a week. It was another thing to make Sannah purple, but I'd have to worry about it later. The ship dove, nose down, sliding steeply into the trough of waves again. As it tipped, my feet went out from under me, and I skidded on my back across the slippery deck.

I scrambled to catch hold of something solid, but there was nothing. Then the ship straightened out, and I came to rest at the foot of the forecastle stairs, right where I needed to be. It was the fastest way I could have gotten there. I grabbed the stair rail, and scrambling up the steps, peeked over at deck-level, just before the next wave hit. There was Checkela, peering out from his place in the coiled rope. Like me, he had no hat. His hair blew wildly in the wind. He was wide-eyed with fear, but so far the box had protected him from the brunt of the waves.

Then the water reared up. My feet slipped on the stairs, but I hung on. I could get to the boy as soon as it passed, as long as he didn't get washed out of the box. The wave passed. I got one foot back under me, and tried to climb. I couldn't move. My shoe was caught between two stairs. I wriggled to get free, but I was off balance. *Come on, come on.* Another wave followed, close on the first, and it looked like a big one.

From where I was, I could just see onto the deck. *Thank goodness*, I breathed. Checkela was still in the box. I could still get him after one more wave. If only he could hang on. If only *I* could hang on. The coming wave was a monster.

Then Checkela did the worst thing possible. He crawled out of the box. Confused by the storm, he turned in stumbling circles, like a drunk on the deck. He could barely stand against the wind.

I shouted for him to get back, but the gale whipped my words out to sea. I could barely hear them myself. And then the wave was upon us. It darkened the sky as the nose of the ship plunged down. I watched helplessly from the stairs. In seconds the water would sweep Checkela away!

Chapter 25

Rescue

I tried again to pull my leg up. Still stuck! The wave was breaking. In desperation, I twisted hard and pulled back. The ribbed steel stair gouged my shin. I leaned back harder, pushing against the stair rails with my hands, and yanked my leg free. Ignoring the pain, I dashed up the stairs, and dove for Checkela. I grabbed him just as the water crashed over us both. We tumbled across the deck. His small arms wrapped around my neck in a stranglehold. His legs were around my waist. I flailed with my arms as we skidded and tumbled, reaching for something—*anything*—to cling to. Water was in my eyes, my mouth, my ears. It seemed, at that moment, like the whole world was made of water. I was sure we had gone over the edge.

Then something hit me like a club across the back, and again on my legs. The water had knocked us against something hard—beams of some sort. Gasping from the blows, I stiffened my body to keep from slipping between them. I reached up with my arms and caught hold of something round—a steel pipe. Terror swept through me. *It was the rail at the edge of the ship!*

"Hang on!" I tried to shout through the water. If Checkela let go, he'd be swept between the rails and gone forever. If my grip slipped, both of us would go.

It seemed like forever before the frenzied water quit trying to tear us from the rail. When it finally subsided, the water had twisted Checkela around, and he was clinging to my side. I stared straight down the steel-plated hull of the ship into a bottomless ocean.

As the deck tipped up and away from the water, I pushed away from the rail, struggling with Checkela. I stumbled and slid back toward the stairs and the main deck, wondering how we would ever make it to safety. But, I reasoned, if that last wave hadn't got us, maybe nothing would.

We made it to the stairs, and to my surprise, a face appeared, and the open arms of a sailor—the same sailor who had offered to whip me to slivers for being out in the storm. This time he seemed glad to see me, but not as glad as I was to see him.

He pried Checkela from around my neck, and threw him under one arm as easily as if he were a feather pillow. Then he slapped me on the back and shouted, "With me. Come!"

We went as I had before, dashing between waves. Each time they hit, the sailor wrapped his burly arms around Checkela and me, holding us to the ropes with crushing strength.

Finally, we tumbled through the hatchway and down the stairs below deck. I fell exhausted, against someone at the bottom. Andreas Vetter. He held me up.

The sound of crying, and sobs of, "Thank God, thank God," filled the hallway. It was Sahra, hugging her son.

The sailor closed the hatch, shutting out the splash and roar of the sea. Everyone hung on as the ship continued to dive and roll with the waves.

"This young man," the sailor's voice boomed out, "has done something foolish beyond words." Everyone gaped in silence. I cringed. Would he whip me to slivers?

"But," the sailor continued, "without such foolishness, the young one here"—he pointed at Checkela—"would be sinking to the depths of the sea even as I speak."

Sahra gasped in horror at the thought, and clung to Checkela even harder.

The sailor shook his head. "Such stubborn courage in one so young, I have never witnessed on the sea."

Andreas' warm hand squeezed my shoulder. "God be praised for his mercy," he said, "and for the stubborn courage of our Paul."

Glancing up, I caught Sannah looking at me, bewilderment softening the stern lines of her face. She stared—strangely, curiously—as if I were some kind of marvelous new machine she did not understand.

It didn't surprise me. I didn't understand myself either. How I had managed to rescue Checkela was too much to figure. Could fear give a person that much strength?

Stubborn courage. That was what they had said. Maybe I was just too stubborn to drown. Whatever it was, it was wearing off fast. As my heart rate returned to normal, I began to shake, remembering the terror of the waves.

Sannah reached a hesitant hand toward me. "God be praised, Paul, for what you have done." Then her hand lighted for a moment on my head. I jumped, expecting her to go after me for losing my hat, but the look in her eye was not anger. Nor was it love. Just a confused holding back of something.

Hannah's mother had nothing to hold back. After hugging Checkela nearly to death, she released him to her husband, and threw herself at me.

"God gave you strength. Thank God he allowed you to be where you were needed. Thank you, Paul, thank you forever, for being so brave."

Her stranglehold was tighter than Checkela's in the storm. I was sure my face was red, if not from embarrassment, then certainly from lack of air. It was a strange thing, but it felt good to be hugged like that. So good, that I almost lost my resolve to not cry. But Sannah Basel saved me.

Spluttering and gagging, Sannah put her hand to her mouth. She doubled over and muttered in misery, "Oh, can someone not stop this awful boat?" Then, with a mighty heave, she splashed her dinner all over the floor.

Chapter 26

Seasick

What happened to Sannah became the plague of almost everyone on the ship. For two days the storm drove the boat over huge waves that rocked and rolled endlessly. We would climb up a wave only to dive wildly down the other side. And we did it over and over, until all we could do was cling to our bunks and groan.

The seasickness was worse for adults than children. Some little ones were especially miserable, though, because their parents were too sick to comfort them.

Anyone who was well enough had to help feed and clean the children, and clean up for the adults who were too sick to move. That meant me, for one. I threw up too, more than once. But I could still eat and stay on my feet. Others were at the point of wishing for death.

All decks were sealed shut to keep the water out. The stink of stale air was enough to make anyone vomit, even without the rocking of the ship. Sailors supplied buckets to our below-deck compartments. Because we were third class passengers, we were crammed tightly into our rooms, with just enough space for the bunk beds we slept in. Though we emptied the buckets regularly, they frothed with the smelly, putrid liquid that slopped over, fouling the air. On top of that, there were hardly any showers, and the smell of unwashed bodies was getting bad.

As I moved through the rooms, collecting and emptying pails, I could hear snatches of prayer, asking for deliverance from the storm. Vomit duty was a horrid job, but the grateful thanks I received encouraged me to keep at it.

I had little time to think about how I had saved Checkela, but the incident increased my prestige with the other kids on board. Some even asked what I thought they should do to help. Mostly, I told them to figure it out for themselves, though I did send Hons Gross to carry vomit buckets in Hannah's place. She had been doing it, until she slipped with the rocking of the ship, and landed on the floor with a bucket on top of her. After that, she said she was going to look after her brother and sisters, and refused to carry any more buckets. I thought Hons might enjoy taking over.

Finally, the storm abated and the sea became smooth again. We cleaned our quarters, and food seemed appealing once more. The decks were flooded, not with water, but with people eager to breathe the fresh air. We gathered together for a *Gebet*, a prayer of thanks to God for safety in the storm.

• • •

"The captain says just a couple more days to New York," Hannah said one afternoon, looking over the bow of the ship to the horizon. We were sitting on the forecastle deck. "The pointer must still be pointing the right way."

"It's not a pointer. It's—"

"It's called the *bowsprit*," Hannah interrupted, mimicking me, "and it's not for pointing. It's where they tie the sails. I heard you two weeks ago, but I still like to call it a pointer. I like to think there's something showing us the way."

"Girls," I sighed.

"Actually, I think Jesus is our pointer, leading us to America. Don't you?"

"Maybe," I replied flatly.

"Don't you think it's exciting that God, who made the whole world, cares about us enough to show us a new place to live?"

"You know my plans," I said with annoyance.

"You can change your plans."

"No, I can't."

"You made them, so you can change them."

"I'm not staying with Sannah."

"I think she is softening toward you."

I had thought so, too, for a moment, just before she threw up. I had wondered what she was holding back. I almost thought it was some feeling for me, but I soon found out it was only the dinner roiling around in her gut. Mind you, she had not been her usual nasty self since then, but maybe she didn't have the energy for it after being so sick.

"How soft can a rock get?" I asked Hannah sarcastically. "Besides, I'll never be her Daniel, will I?"

"You don't have to be her Daniel. Just be who God made you. That person is special. Look how you helped when everyone was sick. People respect that. Even Sannah."

"That was just—"

"And what about my brother? My family will never forget what you did."

"I was just dumb enough to be lucky."

"Before the storm, you said God had no purpose for you. Don't you think he might have proved you wrong?"

"Why?"

"You noticed Checkela. You were there when Mueter came looking, and you got to him just in time. You should have both been drowned, but you weren't. Maybe God had a purpose in bringing you to us, in spite of the way it came about."

"He could have done that with anyone."

"But God chose you, Paul. For whatever reason, you are the one he chose."

I remembered hanging onto the steel cable, and the feeling of assurance that had come over me out of nowhere. I had known I was going to succeed. Even then, it had occurred to me that the assurance might be from God. But I'd had no time to think about it. I did not want to think about it now.

I knew what God thought of me. Besides, there was something about Hannah's way of making herself seem right that annoyed me and made me want to argue.

"If God put me with Sannah for a purpose," I said, "the purpose was punishment. I'm not staying."

"I think you belong with us. It's time to stop feeling sorry for yourself."

Hannah's words stung. "What makes you such a know-it-all? I never asked to go to America. I—" I stopped, realizing the lie. I *had* asked, with that horrible prayer. And it was impossible for Hannah to understand. But I wanted her to. I had been carrying the weight of guilt alone for so long, it was breaking my back.

A breeze ruffled the sails, which were unfurled again, helping the steam engines. The sailcloth snapped like clapping hands, encouraging me to trust her.

My head ached with tension as I worked up the courage to speak. Finally I blurted out, "My parents are dead because of my prayers."

I thought there should have been an earthquake, or a bolt of lightning, but nothing happened. I studied Hannah's face, looking for the disgust I was sure to see. Instead, her deep eyes shone with compassion, making me want to talk. I told her everything, reliving the pain and horror of that awful night. By the time I had finished, sweat dripped from my forehead, and ran down my cheeks like tears. But I did not cry. I was preparing myself for Hannah's rejection.

She said nothing for a long time. Finally, she reached out and took my hand. "Paul," she said, "I know how you feel, and I want to tell you—God has not stopped loving you. It's true, even if you don't believe it."

I thought she would at least know enough to get off my back about God's love when I told her the truth. "No, Hannah, you still don't understand. You can't."

"My father died too, Paul."

"Hannah, I know, but it was different."

"I know God loves me."

"Yes, but—"

"And he loves you too."

"Hannah—"

"Let me finish, Paul. You were honest with me. Maybe I should be honest with you. You see, I didn't tell you my whole story either. When I told you about my father, I left one part out." She paused and took a deep breath. "I didn't tell you that I was the one who killed him."

Chapter 27

Crushed in the Sawmill

I stared at Hannah in disbelief. "But . . . but I thought you said it was the sawmill," I stammered, not sure I had heard her right.

"It was," Hannah replied, straining to keep her voice even. "Maybe I should have told you. Maybe I would have, if I had known what you were going through, but I don't like to remember it."

Shivers of curiosity raced through me, or maybe it was only the vibration of the steam engines at their endless work in the bowels of the ship. Because of the pain in Hannah's voice, I said, "You don't have to tell me if you don't want to."

"No," she replied. "I want you to know God loves you."

"I don't see how—"

"Can't you just listen without arguing?"

I looked across the vast water surrounding our little ship, and prepared to listen.

Hannah began to talk, almost as if to herself, her voice floating between the two blues of sea and sky. "He was saving . . . He was trying to save . . ."

She faltered, then started over. "I liked being there, with the fresh smell of sawdust, and the huffing of the steam engine that ran the mill. It seemed like such a safe place, with the men all working together, cutting the big logs into boards.

"I knew all about it, too. The cantors—that's what my father was—the cantors would roll the logs off the skidway onto a big steel carriage. They fastened them in place with dogs—those are hooks. When the sawyer pushed a lever, the whole carriage slid ahead and ran the logs through the saw blade. Then it came zooming back. I liked watching it. Even the shrieking, big saw didn't scare me. It should have.

"I waited with dinner that day—I had brought it for Fater. There was an old syrup can I was kicking around the yard. It was funny because the saw was so loud, it was like the can didn't make any noise when I kicked it.

"Then the can went under the carriage. I didn't even think. The carriage was stopped for a minute, all the way ahead. I dove under to grab the can. A stupid, *stupid* thing."

Hannah was lost in her memories now, her voice rising from the stirred-up depths of pain.

"All of a sudden the carriage started moving right over my head. The sawyer always stood the other way. He couldn't see me. He was running it back. I crouched down as the cables and pulleys spun past my head. I heard a strange shrieking noise, different from the saw. I realized it was my own scream. But no one else could hear it.

"Something grabbed at my clothes, dragging me along. I fought to get away, but it was no use. It was too strong, digging into my shoulder as if it would rip it off. It slid me along the ground. I knew it would smash me into the carriage frame. I grabbed at an anchor post, and hung on for dear life. I could feel my shirt rip as the machine let go. I had gotten away. But everything was still going, and I couldn't move.

"Then the thing had me again, yanking like a wild beast. It was terrible. How could a machine attack twice the same way? It was like it was alive and coming after me. My shoulder hurt so badly, I couldn't hang on. I screamed as it ripped me loose. Then it tossed me out, clear of the mill."

I looked at Hannah. She was staring straight ahead, out to

the empty water, as if she could see something happening out there. Her hands were clenched tight.

She continued, "That was the other stupid thing. It wasn't the machine that had grabbed me. It was my father. He must have jumped right over the carriage. He had crawled in to save me, and I fought against him.

"He tried to back out. Then it jerked him away.

"The whole thing took just a few seconds. The sawyer turned in time to see my father get caught between a carriage rail and the frame."

Hannah turned to me. Her bright eyes were glassy, and tears glazed her cheeks. "Did you know," she said raggedly, "that a man's legs twitch when he dies?"

A breeze flitted in from the sea, dancing over the deck to ripple Hannah's apron. I wondered how a breeze could be so playful in the face of such a story. The air seemed too thin to breathe, and I felt sick. Not sick for myself, but for Hannah and what she had endured.

"I am twice guilty," she continued. "If I hadn't been so careless, it wouldn't have happened. And if I hadn't fought against him, Fater would have got out."

The picture was alive in my mind. I could see Hannah's horrified face as she watched her father crushed like a matchstick in the mill. And then, in the same picture, I saw my own parents, standing in the grip of a lightning bolt, and a boy watching in horror through a rain-streaked window. I understood then that Hannah knew everything I could ever know about the pain of guilt.

I reached out to her, and put my arms around her thin, strong shoulders, trying to offer some comfort. She was crying quietly.

"I'm sorry, Hannah," I murmured. "Sorry for thinking you didn't know. Sorry for what happened."

"It's okay," she said, straightening her shoulders. "It hurts to tell it, that's all."

"You were only a child, Hannah. You didn't mean any harm. You can't blame yourself."

She breathed deeply, regaining her composure. "There Paul, you've said it. That's what I've been trying to tell you."

My jaw dropped in surprise. The tables had turned again. A second ago, I thought I was comforting a broken girl. But already the light had reappeared in her eyes, and she was trying to help me. "Hannah, where do you get so much strength?" I asked in bewilderment.

"I've been trying to tell you that, too. I took my guilt to Jesus. At first, I thought God would hate me, and I wanted to hate him for letting it happen. But Mueter helped me see I was wrong.

"My father loved Jesus," Hannah continued. "How could I turn my back on the One my father loved? I had to have faith for him."

"I don't think it's that easy."

"Of course it isn't easy. For a long time, I wished I had been the one to die. But I wasn't. I was alive. It was only after Mueter got me to pray—and I prayed lots—that I realized if I spent my whole life hating God, and hating myself, I might as well be dead.

"My father sacrificed his own life to save me. I couldn't waste his final gift. I wanted to make the most of my life for him."

Hannah's talk almost got to me. I remembered my mother's diary. What had she written? *It is my prayer that he will always walk in your truth and your love. What more could a mother ask?*

Maybe for Mueter I would have tried, but who could love in the care of an aunt who destroyed even the book my mother's words were in? It was too much.

Hannah pressed further. "Paul, you know that what my father did is like what Jesus did for all of us. He gave his life to save ours. If you invite Jesus, he'll come in. He'll forgive your sins. All your sins, Paul. You asked where I get my strength. It comes from him."

"You think too much, Hannah. You sound like an old preacher." I smiled to show I was joking, but the joke fell flat.

"Well, you should think a little more. You have to decide if the things that happened will destroy you or make you stronger." Hannah put her hands on my shoulders, pinning me with her deep look. "Paul," she said quietly, "if you like, I could help you start to pray."

For a moment, I almost wanted to. But then, as Hannah had suggested, I started thinking. And all I knew was how much I hated what had happened the last time I prayed. I didn't have it in me to try again. I shook my head. I was about to make an excuse, when another storm blew onto the deck.

"God rebuke such indecent behavior! Remove your hands from one another!" It was Graybeard, stomping across the forecastle. "In broad daylight yet, for all to see!"

I jumped back, as Hannah dropped her hands. I was so surprised I could only gape, like a thief caught stealing.

"Paul, how can you do this? God forbid you should seek advantage for saving her brother."

"It's not what you think," I managed to say.

Hannah tried to explain. "I was asking if he wanted to pray."

"Do not make excuses, girl. I saw him hug you as well. Perhaps some day you will be a great man, Paul, but one noble deed does not excuse indecent behavior. You will receive your correction below. Now come."

Chapter 28

America!

We sighted land, and I could hardly wait for America—and my opportunity. Graybeard's licking hadn't been much, but my pride burned like hot embers under my hide.

Indecent behavior! I remembered the broken wagon reach, and Graybeard holding Sannah's hands with her skirt coming off. Someone should have whipped him.

As if I would try something with Hannah! I hadn't done anything except talk to the only person in the world who half understood me. There was no pleasing these people. They could keep their communal life!

Evening was falling on the fourth of July when we steamed into the new country through an opening called The Narrows. The captain announced that it was Independence Day, and an American on board read from something called the Declaration of Independence. It had been written almost a hundred years before, when the United States decided to separate from England. The Declaration was in English, so I couldn't understand it, but another man said it meant Americans believed God had given every person alive the right to live in freedom and seek happiness.

That boosted my spirits. Freedom and happiness—how good it would be to find them both. Maybe Vanya the Great was right. America sounded like a good place for a new beginning.

As we left The Narrows, the waterway widened into the Upper New York Bay. On the other side was our destination —Manhattan Island. Everyone was on deck. Some were singing, some crying, but all were relieved that the voyage was over. We had been on the *Hammonia* for fifteen days.

The next morning, we boarded a smaller steamer that took us to Castle Garden, a big round building on the tip of Manhattan Island. It had once been a fort, and after that an opera house. Now it was the doorway to America—the immigrant inspection station.

Inside, we were herded around, lined up, and counted for the third time on our journey. Immigration officials checked us for diseases, wrote down our names, and searched our baggage. Then somebody said, "Welcome to America," and we were in. The elders thanked God that no one was turned away.

A railroad land agent named Hiller met us. The railroad companies were eager to sell land to immigrants, so he had been assigned to help us.

Andreas called Hiller a godsend, because nobody among us spoke English.

"Come on," I said to Hannah, grabbing her arm.

"Where?"

"To follow preacher Michael and Graybeard. Hiller is taking them to change the colony's money to American dollars."

"So what?"

"So I'm going to change my money, too. Maybe you can help me." I had taken my parents' Russian rubles from my suitcase before the immigration officers searched it.

"Help you? I don't know anything about it."

"All we have to do," I explained, "is watch what they do, then do the same."

"Can't it wait?"

"This could be my only chance. Come on, before we lose them! Just don't let them see you."

"You're crazy," Hannah said. But she came.

Hiller led the way through the strangest mix of people I had ever seen. Rich and poor, from all countries and religions, jostled against each other in the great, round building. The place was a mad confusion, which made it easy for us to go unnoticed.

Hiller and the elders joined a line leading to a wicket window.

"We need to get close," I said to Hannah.

"Over there," she replied, pointing to a luggage cart near the wicket.

We dodged our way to the far side of the cart, and hid behind it. The elders were almost at the window. Peeking around the baggage, I watched people give money to a man behind the wicket. He would count it, then punch numbers on an adding machine, and give American dollars in return. But it was so noisy, I could not hear what anyone said.

"I need to get closer," I told Hannah.

"What's wrong with watching from here?"

"I need to hear how much it is, so I don't get cheated."

"They'll notice you."

"So what can I do?"

Hannah's hand darted between two suitcases and came out holding an old gray blanket. "Wrap up in this," she said.

"In that?" I asked in disbelief. "I'll look like an idiot."

"You *are* an idiot. Now, hurry up, so we can put it back. And don't worry about your looks. There are people wearing worse than this."

I threw the blanket over my head, and wrapped it around my shoulders as if I had nothing else to wear. I tried to look casual, working my way closer to the wicket, keeping my face turned away.

The money man was telling Hiller something in English. Then Hiller told the preacher in German. He didn't know it, but he told me too. I sneaked back to the luggage cart and darted behind it—planting my nose into the middle of the biggest round stomach I had ever seen.

"I'm sorry," I mumbled in German, stumbling back as a flowery dress came into focus. Looking up, I was confronted by a pair of angry red cheeks, puffing like a blacksmith's bellows, and lips as red as burning coals. Grabbing the blanket, the woman spit sparks and fire that blistered my ears. I had no idea what language she was speaking, but I dreaded to think what names she might be calling me.

As I tried to unwind from the blanket, she yanked it away, spinning me around like a top. It seemed to give her more energy, and she threatened to raise the roof with her ranting.

The crowd was getting thicker around us. Fortunately, the luggage still hid us from the wicket, but our elders would be finished any second. I didn't want Graybeard to find me in the middle of this mix-up. And I couldn't bear to think what would happen if we got arrested. Could a person be thrown out of the country for getting caught borrowing a blanket in the first five minutes? I wondered.

I had to think of something, and quick. Poor Hannah would be worried sick about getting into trouble.

Then she had my hand, pulling me to the floor. "This way, idiot. Follow me."

Crawling on hands and knees through a forest of strange shoes, pant legs, and long dresses, I followed Hannah from the scene of excitement until the shrieking began to fade. There were a few shouts and exclamations along the way, and once I felt a shoe whap my hind end, but no one tried to stop us.

Finally, Hannah stood up, and I with her, trying to look natural, as if crawling around the immigration center was a perfectly normal thing to do. We got some strange looks, but no one was chasing us. Maybe nobody else understood the woman either. Or maybe these things happened here all the time. The important thing was, neither the preacher nor

Graybeard had seen us.

"Why is it," Hannah complained, catching her breath, "that every time I go somewhere with you, it means trouble? Next time I hear you say, 'Come on,' I'm staying put."

"Come on," I replied. "Hiller said you get forty-three cents for every ruble."

"After all that, you're still going to change your money?"

"I told you—it might be my only chance."

"And I told you—you're an idiot. Remember?"

"Come on. You can't stay here alone. It's dangerous for a girl."

Chapter 29

The Navy Colt

"*Ach*, these Americans are a marvel with the things they build." Andreas Vetter was talking to Jacob Stahl. He was almost shouting, to make himself heard in the clattery tunnel. We were starting our journey with a twenty-minute train ride under the Hudson River, on our way to Lincoln, Nebraska. The air was sooty from the locomotive fire.

On the floor of the crowded carriage, dimly lit by built-in gas lanterns, Hannah chuckled softly about our escape from the screaming lady.

"You would have thought someone was being murdered," she said, shaking her head. "Such a fuss over an old blanket. I thought sure the man at the money window was questioning you for it."

"*Joh*, my heart almost stopped," I replied, remembering. When I had handed my money to the man in the window, he had counted it and started jabbering away in English. I tried to tell him in German and in Russian that I wanted forty-three cents each for my rubles, but he just banged his hand loudly on the counter and stomped away.

He came back with another man. This man had a scowling face, but he spoke German.

"Whose money is that?" he demanded.

"It's, uh—"

"Since when does a boy have so much money? Speak up!"

"I, uh, it belongs to my parents," I answered, trying to be as truthful as possible.

"Why are they not changing it themselves?"

"Because they can't," I replied.

"Why can they not?"

I was sure he would call a guard and accuse me of stealing. If he did, I would have to get Sannah or Andreas, or maybe Graybeard. I shuddered to think how complicated that could get. I gave the only reply I could. "Because both of them have been laid low. They cannot get up. The train is going soon, and it is up to me to get the money changed."

His eyes bored holes into me, trying to see if I was telling the truth. I hated what I'd said about my parents, but the words were true, even if it wasn't exactly the way I'd made it sound. I wasn't doing anything illegal, so I met the man's gaze squarely.

People in line jostled against me. They were getting impatient. Finally, the German-speaking man shrugged his shoulders in exasperation and said something in English. The other man punched numbers into the adding machine, and gave me 215 American dollars.

Hannah's soft voice returned me to the present. "I think life is simpler without so much money."

"*Joh*," I replied, wiggling my foot, "but it sure makes good padding in the shoe."

• • •

It seemed like we had been traveling forever, first across the vast lands of Russia and Europe, then over the great Atlantic Ocean, and now into the heart of North America. Everyone was tired, and some of the smaller children were crying and getting sick.

Our train snaked through New York state to Buffalo, over a

piece of Ontario, Canada, and then across a ferry to Detroit. After a short stop in Chicago, we headed west through Illinois until we crossed the mighty Mississippi River at Burlington, Iowa. On the fifth day, on Iowa's western border, the tracks ran right up to the wide waters of the Missouri River and stopped.

Because so many settlers in Iowa and Nebraska had come from Germany, we had no trouble finding people to explain where we were and what was going on.

"We can get out at this station for a little while," Preacher Waldner announced, after talking to someone in the car ahead of us. "We must wait for the steamboat ferry to come across the river. The city of Plattsmouth, Nebraska, is on the other side, and Lincoln is only fifty miles beyond it."

We piled out of the railcar and saw a sidetrack, a water tower, and fuel sheds for the locomotives. People waited by the dock with wagons and horses.

"Lukas Hartmann, *Du brauchst eine Frau.*" I heard a snatch of German among the English talk. "You need a wife," an older man said to a younger one, chuckling. They were standing by an empty wagon. I wandered in their direction, more interested in the way they looked than in their language. The two men wore high boots and wide, Western hats. Most intriguing of all was the brown-handled gun that hung from the younger one's hip. I had seen a few guns from the train window, but none this close. I edged in for a better look, and to listen to their talk. But they had switched to English.

The younger one noticed me, and said something. I stood like a ninny, staring at his gun. He said something else. I couldn't understand the English, but I could tell he was annoyed with me for not answering.

"*Ich röd nit Englisch,*" I answered—"I don't speak English."

"So," the older man said in German, "from the old country. And right off the boat too, I would say. How do you like America?"

I shrugged. "From the train, it looks like a fine country for an adventure."

"*Ach*, adventure," he laughed, looking at the younger man. "My nephew, too, thinks he needs more adventure. But a man is better off finding work."

"*Joh*," I said eagerly, "I would like to find work."

"Then you will do well for yourself," he said with a smile.

The man seemed so friendly, I wondered if he could tell me where to start. I had told Hannah I was going to run away, but I was lost in this strange, English-speaking world. "Can you tell me what work there is to do?" I asked nervously.

"Homesteading," the man replied. "It's filling up here, but tell your father to keep going west. He will find his land."

"My father is dead. I'm with some other people, but I need to get out and work."

"Hmm, fallen on hard times, have you? You might try to find work on a ranch—maybe one like mine." He looked thoughtful. "My nephew and I are waiting for a load of fencing supplies coming over from Plattsmouth. But that is hard work for a boy your age."

Just then two blasts from a steam whistle sounded across the water. "Now wait a minute," the man said. "Maybe that's your answer. Do you see that fancy old side-wheeler?"

A riverboat was churning through the muddy waters of the Missouri.

"It's called the *Astrid Wilhemina*. Perhaps Captain Braun would be willing to hire a cabin boy."

"But who is—?"

"Captain Adam Braun has been a riverboat captain for twenty years. He started in the glory days of the riverboat. There are not so many now, with the railroad taking over, but there are still some that keep busy."

"But how can I—?"

"Captain Braun works the river between St. Louis and

Sioux City. He will be down from Sioux City in two days, then up again from St. Louis in another six. He speaks German, so you tell him Dieter Hartmann sent you. He is an old friend, and might just sign you on."

Dieter Hartmann spoke so quickly, listing the things I should do, that my head was spinning. "Yes, I . . . Thank you," I stammered.

"Just be sure to look for the *Astrid Wilhemina*."

I must have still been staring at the younger man's gun because he asked, "You like guns, do you?" He seemed more relaxed than at first.

"I, uh, I've never actually seen one close up before. Our people don't allow them."

The young fellow laughed. "If you're going to be an adventurer, you should have a gun." He took it out of its holster, and held it out to me, handle first. The gun had a long, six-sided barrel. "Here, maybe you'd like to have a look at it. It's called a Navy Colt."

"Lukas, do not put ideas in his head," Dieter cautioned. "Look if you like, young man, but remember, a gun is a tool, not an adventurer's toy. Sometimes we need one on the ranch."

Handling a gun was not for us Hutterites. Still, I could see nothing wrong with having a look. I reached a guilty hand toward the gun. My fingers were just sliding over the handle when the screaming started.

Chapter 30

Riverboat

The screaming came from Sannah. She hated guns.

"Is it not enough to be constantly in trouble?" she cried. "Is it not enough to be constantly disrespectful? Is it not enough to be drawn to every worldly attraction? Now you want guns as well?" Her legs pumped like steam pistons, jerking her apron as she stormed across the ferry dock. She grabbed my ear and marched off the way she had come, dragging me behind her.

"Are you so devilish you want to be a gunfighter? Is it too much for you to be a Hutterite?"

I heard the laughter of the Hartmanns. The whole train was watching. Both my ear and my pride were burning. "Is it too much for you that I am not your own little Daniel?" I shouted, letting my anger loose. "No wonder he died. He had to get away from you!"

I should never have been so cruel. Mueter would have been dismayed. Fater would have been furious. But just then I hated Sannah Basel like fire. She let go of my ear as if it had burned her fingers. Then she walked stiffly away to the water by herself.

Graybeard was coming, slow and stern, but Andreas Vetter stopped him with words I could not hear. Then he approached, and looked me in the eye. "You should not have hurt your

147

Basel that way, Paul. She is sometimes harsh, but such words of yours are poison. God forgive you both for such tempers. I want no more of this. Now watch the ferry come, and turn your thoughts to God."

I had no trouble watching the ferry come. I had no trouble watching the locomotive push our train coach down the track and onto the ferry deck. But I *did* have trouble turning my thoughts to God. If he loved me so much, why couldn't he get me out of this hateful situation?

Yes, Sannah, maybe it is too much for me to be a Hutterite, I thought, *especially with you.* I turned my heart to stone. I was as good as gone.

• • •

Immigrants were pouring into Nebraska. A land agent told us it had been part of the Indian Territory just twenty years before. Then, whites had only passed through on the Oregon Trail. But soon the Indians were pushed back as white settlers started oozing in. Then the railroad arrived and the land rush went crazy. From a lawless western outpost, Lincoln, Nebraska, became a thriving boomtown and state capital. For us, it turned into a city of disaster.

The boarding houses and hotels in Lincoln had no rooms available, especially for a group of more than 230 people. Finally, someone set us up in an old barn at the edge of town, and local people donated boards to lay across the floor so we could sleep above the dirt. It wasn't much, but at least our beds were not on water or wheels. We had been traveling almost every day for over a month. Everyone was exhausted.

While six of our elders searched the country for good land to start a colony, the other men went into the city to look for day jobs. Everyone settled in for a lengthy stay. Everyone except me.

Already, on the first day, something disturbing was happening. Several children were sick with violent, bloody diarrhea. They became so weak and feverish they hardly knew who they were.

I couldn't do anything to help them, so on the first morning I took my chance to sneak away. Before anyone was up, I ducked out of our building, and crossed the street in the direction of the railroad station.

I figured people would be distracted by the sickness, and I would not be missed. Sannah would be angry, but then, she would be angry even if I stayed. Maybe Andreas would have regrets, but he would soon get over them. Still, my own sadness over leaving Andreas surprised me. He had been kind.

Hannah was the hardest. I wanted to say good-bye, but didn't know how. She had become more than a friend. Almost a sister, or . . . or who knows what? Tears filled my eyes. I felt frightened and alone. But if America was to be my land of new beginnings, there had to be endings as well. I hoped Hannah would understand.

When I was almost out of earshot, a shriek went up from our old wooden building. "My baby, my little baby Maria!" The cry was so desolate, I knew one of the children had died. I covered my ears, and walked stiffly toward the train.

• • •

Just as Dieter Hartmann had promised, the *Astrid Wilhemina* stopped at Plattsmouth on its return from Sioux City, and Captain Braun was German. Unfortunately, I could understand him clearly.

"*Ach*, no! What do I need with a cabin boy? I have one, and a good one at that. Good-bye."

But when I told him Dieter Hartmann had sent me, he scratched his whiskers and seemed to think about it. When I added that I would work free for a month, so he could see if I was any good, he stopped scratching and agreed.

"But I warn you," he said, "if you have come only to watch the river go by, I will put you off at the first stop."

As the *Astrid Wilhemina* steamed downstream toward St. Louis, Missouri, I found myself up on her top deck with a paint bucket in one hand and a brush in the other. In the blistering sun, I painted the pilothouse, a little building on top of the crew's quarters, from which the captain steered the boat. The pilothouse was on top of the Texas deck, which was on a bigger deck called the hurricane deck. All of that was just the top part of the boat. Underneath it were the boiler deck and the main deck, with passenger cabins and the gaming room. I was painting my way down to the hurricane deck.

• • •

"You mean you didn't even know you were getting on a gambling boat?" Florian, the cabin boy, asked, shaking his head in wonderment. It turned out that gambling was one of the boat's main attractions. Sannah would think I had gone completely wicked now.

"How would I know?" I said. "I've never even *seen* a riverboat before."

The cabin boy was also a German. He wasn't really a boy, but was skinny, with a bent leg that looked as if it hadn't grown properly. Florian said he was eighteen years old, and he liked working on the riverboat because of the interesting people he met. He seemed glad to have me to talk to.

During the day, I worked almost nonstop to prove myself. In the evenings I talked with Florian, watched the river go by, and sometimes cried myself to sleep. *Paul Wipf.* That was my name, but who was I? My world seemed to get more and more out of joint.

One evening, Florian said excitedly, "You won't believe who we have on board! Come with me, and I'll show you something to tell your grandchildren about."

He led the way to the boiler deck and into the elegant gambling room. "Over there," he said. "Standing by the counter. See him?"

As my eyes adjusted to the lantern light in the room, I saw him standing by the bar. The first thing that caught my eye was the bright red sash around his middle. Tucked into the sash were two large, pearl-handled revolvers.

"Navy Colts," I whispered in awe.

Florian was surprised. "You know guns?"

"I saw one a few days ago. It's the only gun I know. But these are fancier."

The man's clothes looked expensive. He had a long coat, and his blond hair hung long and wavy under a black hat with a wide round brim. His drooping mustache and confident stance made him look dashing and handsome. "Now that," I murmured quietly, "is a man to admire."

"Do you know who he is?" Florian asked.

"No, who?"

"The most famous gunfighter alive—Wild Bill Hickok."

Chapter 31
Wild Bill

The next few days, I watched Wild Bill every chance I got. Each evening found him in the gambling room, drinking and playing cards. At first I couldn't get over what a wonderful man he was. His gray eyes reminded me of a hawk—sharp, and missing nothing. He sat with his back to the wall, always watching the room. The card games were sometimes tense, but none of the other players uttered a word against him. I was sure Wild Bill had never put up with scoldings from an aunt who didn't like him—or from anyone else, either. I doubted he was afraid of anyone.

Florian told me all about him.

"The newspapers say he's killed over a hundred men."

"A hundred?" I repeated in disbelief.

"Sure, but it's probably not more than a dozen or two. He's been known to stretch the truth."

I felt a chill in my bones. A dozen human beings, a dozen lives. It was hard to imagine how he could do so much killing. *Could such a man have any fear of God?* I wondered. *Or any love inside him?*

"He used to be a lawman, but he didn't keep a job for long," Florian explained. "He was too quick to kill. Most people can't stomach his methods."

I noticed that Wild Bill liked to drink. At first, he seemed to know what he was doing, but that was in the evenings. By late night, he was a stumbling drunk. Once, when something woke me before dawn, I crept from my cabin to the hurricane deck. Peering over the edge to the boiler deck below, I could just make out the shadow of a man leaning over the rail. It was Wild Bill. He was vomiting into the Missouri. Why would such a man become a drunk like that? I became less sure of my admiration. Still, Wild Bill Hickok was a fine sight to see in the afternoon and evening.

It was on the first night of our return trip from St. Louis that the nightmare began. Wild Bill was still on the boat. Florian, who was constantly eavesdropping, had said Wild Bill was staying on to fatten his wallet with other gamblers' money. I wondered why, since it looked to me like he lost more than he won.

That night I was polishing the brass handrail to the stairs as an excuse to be in the gambling room. Its plush walls absorbed the murmur of voices floating out from the tables. The scene was so serene, it might have been a prayer meeting. I took pleasure in the quiet. It had been a strange day for me, first seeming too hot, then suddenly too cold. Strange Missouri weather, I supposed. I was unbelievably tired.

I had hoped to talk with Wild Bill sometime, but he was not an approachable man. His hard eyes were like a barrier between him and the world, and I doubted that even his friends got close. Though he smiled and sometimes laughed, I found myself wondering whether he was happy inside. Oh, but it was hot!

As I stared at Wild Bill's table, my imagination put another man beside him. It was my own dear father, though he would never wish to be at such a table, even in someone's imagination. He was not handsome like Wild Bill, or richly dressed like Wild Bill, and he had no fancy guns like Wild Bill. What I saw in my father—*remembered,* actually—was an inside strength. It was not a strength for fighting and killing, but a strength for living, a deep strength that had room for love. It shone through his eyes. What I saw was a better man than Wild Bill. I felt Fater was asking me, *What kind of man will you be? Where are you headed now?* I shook off the vision with a shiver. Why was it so chilly in here?

Crash! The sound of breaking glass startled me so badly I spilled brass polish on the hardwood floor. Leaning over a table, a cowboy was leveling his gun at a man in a round bowler hat—a professional gambler. The cowboy's chair had fallen over backwards, and glass from a broken bottle lay scattered on the floor. He was shouting something about the cards. I had learned enough English to recognize cussing, and the word, "cheat." There was only a small amount of money where the cowboy had sat. But the gambler had lots.

At that moment I wouldn't have been the gambler for anything. But he didn't look worried. He just sat there, staring coldly at the cowboy.

Glancing at Wild Bill's table, I saw that one of the ivory-handled revolvers had appeared in his hand. His eyes were terrifying, like a hawk's before it rips into a prairie dog. Something in those cold eyes seemed almost not human, like something that wanted to kill.

Quiet now, the cowboy spit menacingly on the table. Then everything seemed to move slowly, though it was over in a second. The cowboy cocked his gun with his thumb, and a ripping *boom* shattered the night. Splinters flew from the table like feathers lifting in a wind. The cowboy reeled backwards, his gun tipping up toward the ceiling. Another boom chased the echo of the first, and the chandelier shattered. Clutching his stomach, the cowboy fell to the floor. Still, the gambler did not move.

My brain reeled with confusion. The wrong man had fallen. Then as Wild Bill stood, and Captain Braun burst into the room, the gambler brought his hand from under the table and laid a gun on top of it. So that was it—he had shot the cowboy right through the table! No wonder the splinters had flown. The cowboy had never even known the gambler had a gun.

The gambler held up his hands and shrugged as if to say, "I had no choice."

It was hot again in the room. The cowboy groaned sickeningly. It was horrible. Was this how men became heroes? By fighting over a card game for money, by shooting open someone's stomach from under a table? I felt dizzy. My, but it was hot!

My stomach knotted up, and I started to drool. I ran out through the big doorway to the boiler deck and fresh air. As Wild Bill had done before, I leaned my slobbery head over the rail, and vomited into the Missouri.

The next thing I knew, things were gurgling lower down, and I had to run for the toilet. I was cramping up something fierce inside. I doubled over and clutched my stomach so tightly, I must have looked like the one who'd been shot. Desperately trying to hold myself together, I scrambled to the *head*—the toilet on the boat. I made it just in time.

I was desperately sick. The raging diarrhea turned me inside out. Even after half an hour, I couldn't leave the head. An awful pain knotted me up inside. I was sweating like a horse, then chills raced up and down my spine.

Weakness settled on me, like a heavy shroud. I wondered, *Did the shooting upset me this much?* The little room whirled dizzily. I had to get out. Everything was getting blurry. Hoisting up my pants, I stumbled through the doorway, and the hardwood decking raced up to meet my face.

Chapter 32

Epidemic

Everything was a blur—of dreams, voices, and strange shapes floating by. Sometimes a coolness wiped over my face, and bits of sound drifted into my world. *Dysentery. Can he last much longer? Not much of a prayer. Contact his family?* Sliding between oblivion and pain, I wondered who they could be talking about.

Finally, a familiar voice filtered through the confusion, strong and gentle. I thought it was my father. Had he come to forgive me? I was floating. A ceiling drifted by, then opened into sunshine. Hands carried me along. Then the lights went out again.

• • •

Restless images raced through my thoughts, whirling and fading away like debris in a buran wind. I didn't know whether I was thinking or dreaming, but every image came with a question that needed an answer. The old Jewish man, with his wild mat of hair, was there, laughing his bitter laugh, alone and unforgiving in his craziness, forever in the shadow of his dead sons' graves. *Do you know where you are going?* he asked. There was Vanya the Great, con artist and thief, with his juggling balls and samogon. Was it true, as he said, that the family I had was better than no family at all? And there was Wild Bill Hickok, the hard-eyed gunfighter, fearing no one and needing no one. How many times had he done what I saw the gambler do? Was he really a hero?

Through it all, my father asked, *What kind of man will you be, Paul?*

I don't know, Fater.

Will you be a man who knows how to love?

I want to be, Fater, I want to be. But you know what I did to you. How can I be free of it?

Just let me love you.

How can you love me, Fater?

Jesus, my Jesus.

I woke to the sound of soft weeping. I could hear it right beside me. Opening my eyes a crack, I saw a high ceiling of old, weathered boards. My eyelids were so heavy I had to let them fall shut, but the chills and hot rushes were gone. Where was I?

"Just let me love you. Just let me love. Jesus, oh Jesus," someone moaned.

Then slowly it made sense. I had been sick. I must have been desperately sick. I remembered train whistles, and a jostling and rocking. There had been prayers in Hutterite German, and there was the high ceiling above me. Somehow, I was back in the barn.

The crying was familiar. Sannah Basel. At least her voice was familiar, but I had never heard her weep like this. I wondered what was wrong. Was she crying because I had returned?

"Forgive me, Father," Sannah was praying. "On my knees, I ask you—help me to love." Then there was quiet, and footsteps approaching on the boards. Struggling against sleep, I tried to listen.

"Is he . . .? We have not lost him, have we?" It was Andreas Vetter. His voice sounded husky.

"The fever has broken."

"God be praised for his mercy." A big hand brushed my forehead. "Paul, son Paul."

Son Paul? I had not heard those words since Mueter and Fater died.

"Andreas," Sannah was saying, "I have been wrong, so wrong. I have been awful to Paul. Because of my own hard heart, I could not even recognize his grief. You tried to tell me, but I would not listen."

What? Had Sannah lost her mind, or was mine playing tricks?

She continued. "How could I have expected him to accept a new life with us, when I refused to love him? Andreas, I have seen my reflection, and I do not like what I have seen."

"Your reflection, Sannah?"

"Do you remember when Paul shouted that Daniel probably died to escape me?"

"I heard it," Andreas answered.

"It was a slap to my face. My Daniel was happy. He had all my love. Then I walked to the river, and saw my own distorted reflection in the water. And I knew—how different was the woman Paul saw from the mother Daniel had known. Never once had I shown love for Paul. There was no love in me to give." She was crying again.

"Sannah," Andreas said, "God will replenish your love."

"I have asked him, if it is not too late. I drove Paul away, Andreas. I drove him almost to destruction. I loved our Daniel too much, Andreas, and I quit loving altogether when he died. But look at the pain my empty heart has caused. What if, in the horror of this place, everyone became like me? Could any of us claim to be God's people?"

I wondered what horror she was talking about.

"Sannah, do not torture yourself," Andreas replied.

"No, Andreas, you do not understand. It was terrible to see what I've become. I cannot stand it any longer. God give me the courage to change."

Then she started talking about me again. "When Paul ran away, the guilt was like a nail in my heart. But when you answered the telegram and brought him back so sick, I realized something else."

So it was Andreas I had thought was my father. Florian must have told the captain I had come from the Hutterites in Lincoln.

"I realized I had come to admire Paul's courage. He has a good heart, but I would not see it, or recognize how terribly he was hurting. I could have loved him and helped him had I not been so cold, so afraid. Then I thought it was too late." Sannah's sobbing stopped her words.

"Perhaps you will have another chance," Andreas said, his voice choking.

"May God make it so. When Paul came to us, I thought we were doing him a great favor," Sannah said. "I had no idea it was I who needed *him*. God is using him to help me find healing."

"Perhaps we all need one another," Andreas replied soothingly.

Was this the Sannah Basel I knew? A sigh escaped my lips as sleep dragged me away. Maybe I was still lost in delirium.

• • •

When I recovered enough to stay awake, I wished I were still delirious. Eighty-year-old Darius Stahl and thirty-four children were dead. That was the horror Sannah had been talking about.

The dysentery epidemic had just begun when I ran away with the deadly germs already in my body. The first infection had probably come from somewhere else on the trip, but in the unsanitary conditions of the old barn, it spread like fire, especially among the children. Even red-haired Hons Gross had died.

"Where is Hannah?" I asked, realizing I had not seen her. Andreas grew quiet. A fingernail of fear scratched inside me. "Where is Hannah?" I repeated, trying to sit up.

"With her mother," Andreas said quickly, pressing me onto the mat that served as my bed on the floor. "She is sick."

I felt as if a pile of bricks was crushing me. "No, no," I moaned, looking from side to side through the great, open room. "Not Hannah."

Black kerchiefs bobbed here and there above the mats, as women cared for the sick. Low moans and occasional sobs drifted through the sickly stench.

"How sick?" I asked.

"Her life is in the hands of the Lord," Andreas replied.

Chapter 33

Hannah

By the next day, I was able to get up. But, oh, how weak I felt. I had to drink lots of water to replace lost fluids.

I was not prepared to see Hannah so sick, but I shouldn't have been shocked. Everywhere, children and the elderly groaned on their beds. Numbers thirty-six and thirty-seven had died since my recovery.

"Hannah," I whispered, kneeling down beside her. Her face glistened with sweat, and her hair was damp and stringy. Her eyes seemed even larger in her sunken face. They lit up for a moment when she saw me.

"Paul. I'm so glad," she murmured, barely moving her lips. "I prayed . . . to save you from the khappers." Then she was mumbling more nonsense. Her breathing rattled like old bones.

At that moment, I realized just how much Hannah meant to me. Even when I had run away to the riverboat, I didn't really know. I thought back to how she had driven me crazy when we first met, refusing to leave me alone. But without her, I would probably be as crazy by now as the old Jewish man in the cart. There was no one as kind or as wise or as fun as my Hannah. I knew she was the best friend anyone could have.

"Hannah," I said, "I'll do anything to help you." But she

was unconscious. There was nothing I could do.

Back at my mat, I thought about all that had happened. Was it possible that Hannah was right—that God had a purpose in all things? Because of her father's death, Hannah had greater faith and wisdom than most people twice her age. *The things that happen can make you stronger or destroy you*, she had said.

Hannah had turned to God so her father's sacrifice would not be wasted. I knew my parents would want me to turn to God, too. Hannah kept urging me to pray. Maybe I could try, if only for them. If only for Hannah.

That evening, I lay on my mat and tried to recite one of the old Hutterite prayers I had memorized, but the words sounded hollow. They were not about me or the things on my heart. I tried my own prayer, but I was so rusty, I didn't know where to begin. Something in me still fought against God.

I remembered Andreas' buran story, in the windmill. "Jesus is your miller," he had told me.

Finally, I said, "Jesus, if you want to hear from me, please help me speak." I said it over and over, until at last a sense of calm overcame my resistance, and I started talking to God. I confessed my selfishness about wanting to go to America, I confessed hating communal life, and hating Sannah Basel. I asked for forgiveness, and for help to understand the troubles of this life.

At first, nothing changed. There were no angry thunderbolts or starbursts of joy—just me talking. But gradually, a feeling crept over me that I was not alone, a feeling that someone understood.

But when I got to Hannah, I stumbled. A doctor had visited her earlier and said she would probably not last the night. I so wanted her to live, but I was afraid to pray. Could I trust God?

For some reason, I went to Andreas. Maybe it was because

no matter how much I had fought him, he always seemed to care. It was time to tell my story again.

Sannah came along just as I started. Andreas asked her to stay. At first, I didn't want her there, but decided I would at least find out if she meant what I had overheard the night before.

I described everything in detail, from my prayer to go to America, to the sizzling blue of the horrible lightning bolt. Through gritted teeth, I told my story, refusing to break down.

Sannah, I had to admit, seemed like a different person. I expected her to say I got what I deserved with such godless prayers, but she didn't. She sat with her hands in her lap, and tears slipping down her cheeks. Something had softened her. It was the second time she had cried in two days.

Andreas Vetter put his strong hand on my shoulder, and looked into my eyes. It was strange how he reminded me of my father. "You must not think that your prayer has killed your parents," he said. "God is not demented. He would not answer an innocent prayer in such a twisted way. God knows you loved your parents, Paul."

When I said nothing, Andreas raised his eyebrows. "Ah, Paul," he said, "I believe you are afraid you did not love them well enough."

As soon as he said it, I knew he was right. "But I wanted to go to America, even if they didn't," I blurted.

"Paul! You must leave that thinking. Does wanting America mean you did not love your parents? Look around this room. There are many wives here who did *not* want to come to America. They had to come with their husbands, but that does not mean their husbands do not love them. There are parents in this room whose children have died because they came to America, but does that mean they did not love their children? No! Such things happen, and we cannot always tell why."

"But it was my prayer—"

"No, Paul. A Hutterite believes that when it is time for a man to die, he will die. God's ways are so much higher than ours, sometimes they do not make sense to us. It is hard for us to accept, but perhaps it was your parents' time, Paul. Perhaps God allowed it to happen in a way that would make you stronger than you might have been otherwise. Paul, do not blame God for what you do not understand. And do not blame yourself for something you did not cause."

He patted my shoulder and said finally, "Now, is there not someone else you would like to pray for?"

I nodded. "But what if I pray for Hannah, and she dies?" I asked, caught again by my fear.

"Paul, listen. God may answer your prayer for Hannah in the way you hope, and he may not. But he will never do harm just because of your prayers. You must remember that."

"But if a Hutterite believes a person will die when it is time to die, what's the use of praying?"

"Perhaps it *is* Hannah's time. But, Paul, we do not know God's purposes. Perhaps he is only waiting to answer your prayers."

We knelt, then, and did what would have been impossible only a few days before. The three of us prayed together, Sannah Basel, Andreas Vetter, and I. Maybe God already knew how it would go with Hannah, but I decided to do my part. We poured it all out for Hannah, and something unexpected happened as we did. I had the feeling the three of us were praying ourselves into a family.

When we finished, I got the surprise of my life. Sannah stood up and nearly hugged the breath out of me. Then she said, "Paul, I hope you will forgive me. You have gone through too much, including having a harsh old woman to put up with. I didn't know how hard it was for you. I didn't want to know. But if you let me, I will try to make a difference, for you and for all of us."

I didn't know what to say, except that maybe I hadn't been perfect either, and maybe we could start with forgiving each other.

When she kissed my cheek, my determination dissolved into thin air. There she was, crying again. And I was crying with her.

Chapter 34

The Day of Gifts

In the days that followed, everyone felt pain and loss. Thirty-six children and one old man were dead. It was strange how suffering could either bring people together or tear them apart. The epidemic worked like glue among the communal Hutterites, and maybe it was sharing the sorrow that helped draw me in. Suddenly there were many others who understood the anguish I had known. And because I had suffered already, I could help others now.

I had hated these people at first, but I'd hated myself then, too. My own family was gone forever, but there was hope for my relationship with Sannah and Andreas.

Things were not perfect. Old ways died hard, and sometimes the sparks still flew. But it was getting easier all the time to talk things out, and pray. I started praying a lot.

• • •

The day of gifts came three days after my talk with Sannah and Andreas. I found the first gift by my bed when I awoke. A wooden cigar case rested next to my head—my mother's treasure box! Inside were her diary and the small, brass cross. With shaky fingers, I popped open the cross. There was my father's strong face, and Mueter, with her secret smile—a smile just for me.

I felt eyes watching me, and looked around. A few beds away, Sannah Basel sat on a wooden crate. She came to me, a smile playing on her lips. It was strange how she was changing. I hadn't noticed before, but in her smile I could see a resemblance to my mother.

"I thought you burned it," I said in disbelief.

"I was going to, but in the end, I could not," she replied.

"You want me to have it?"

She hesitated, as if in thought. "You know we do not believe in crosses or photographs." Then she quoted from the second commandment. "'You shall not make for yourselves an idol in the form of anything in heaven above or on the earth beneath or in the waters below. You shall not bow down to them or worship them.'

"Paul, when I took the cross from you, I planned to burn it and, in my anger, the diary with it. But between endless train rides and lost baggage cars in Russia, I had no chance. Then I decided I would throw it into the ocean from our ship, but something stopped me. Something said these things are not objects of worship. I believe the Lord would have you keep these reminders of your Mueter and Fater. I am sorry for taking them away."

"Thank you," I said gratefully. Sannah's openness reminded me of something I needed to say. "There was more in the box," I confessed.

"What do you mean?" Sannah asked.

Reaching for my shoe, I slipped out the innersole, and removed four slightly worn fifty-dollar bills. "There were five hundred rubles too," I said. "I kept them to help me run away."

Her jaw dropped in shock. "You were planning it even then?"

I shrugged. "I guess I should turn it over to the colony. I don't want to run away anymore."

For a long time, Sannah did not reply. Finally she said, "Paul, in community we do not keep money for ourselves, but perhaps, if I explain everything to Preacher Michael, we can put this money away until you are old enough to decide for sure. If you go your own way, it will help you get started. If you decide your home is with us, you can give it to the community then."

That was the second gift.

The gift most precious was the third—Hannah. She was with me now, rocking and jostling on the seat beside me, to the familiar clickety-clack of the rails.

"So what do you want to do for excitement?" she yawned.

"I don't think we'll find much excitement on this train, Hannah."

"Maybe not, but that shouldn't stop you. Maybe you'd like to get out and run alongside for a while."

"Only if you come with me," I joked.

"Going places with you gets me in too much trouble."

"Then it's lucky for you I'm not going anywhere."

"Hah! Are you sure you won't run off to become a juggler, or a sailor? Or maybe you'd like to go gunfighting with Wild Bill Hickok. Crazy Paul and Wild Bill—wouldn't that be a good team?" she giggled.

"Then you'd be our Calamity Jane," I replied.

"Calamity Jane? Who's that?"

"Oh, just a wild cowgirl who reminds me of you."

"Very funny. How do you know people like that?"

"A fellow named Florian told me about her."

"Who's Florian?"

"It's a long story. I'll tell you all about it sometime."

"I'm sure you will. You have enough hot air to tell stories till you're a hundred."

That was Hannah. Full of wisecracks already. I was glad to have her back. When she emerged from her fever, I thought the angels were blowing trumpets of joy. Her first smile was like heaven shining on me. In fact, it was like heaven shining on all of us, because it ended the dying. When Hannah recovered, the epidemic was over.

• • •

Black soot fluttered past my carriage window from the smokestack of the locomotive engine. I watched silently for a while, as towering thunderheads gathered in the sky.

"There's going to be a storm, Hannah," I said.

I turned to see why she did not reply, and a last slanting ray of sunlight blazed out from under the clouds. Through the window it lit up Hannah's chestnut hair, and danced on the beauty of her face. She was sleeping. Still weak from her illness, she needed her rest. She'd get plenty of that soon. This was the last train ride.

After almost a month in Nebraska, we had finally left it behind. Our elders had decided the land was too dry. Because the sick could not travel, six men had gone up to the Dakota Territory alone. They found good land, with rolling prairie and long grass that reminded them of the Russian steppes, and sent word for the rest of us to come.

Darkness fell, and the rain fell with it. I watched through the water-streaked window as lightning shredded the Dakota night, bolt after bolt slashing the fabric of the sky. The storm was awesome in power, but I was not afraid.

Much had happened since that other night by a rain-streaked window when my world turned upside down. I would not have wished my experience on anyone. Yet, coming through it, I knew I was a better person than before. And maybe some good had come to Sannah Basel and Andreas Vetter too.

I thought again of the question from the old man in Russia: *Do you know where you are going?* I finally had an answer.

Maybe all of life was a journey. But it didn't matter where you traveled, or who traveled with you. Communal, non-communal, Russia, America—it made no difference, as long as your path was paved with the love of Christ.

With this thought, a deeper peace than I had ever known settled upon me, and as another blast of lightning ripped the sky like a veil, I knew. I knew beyond doubt that at the end of my journey I would see my parents again, when all those who loved the Lord were united in glory.

Afterword

Fact or fiction?

This novel is not a detailed travelogue of the Hutterite migration to America, but it is accurate as to time, place, and major events. The route, time line, and place names are all part of the historical record, as are the story of the *khappers*, disappearing baggage cars, sailing on the *Hammonia*, a storm at sea, and the devastating dysentery epidemic in Nebraska. I have done my best to accurately represent Hutterite history, life, and beliefs, and apologize for those instances where I have missed the mark.

Michael Waldner and Darius Walter, the preachers, and Hiller, the rail company agent, are historical figures. Most other characters are purely fictional, bearing no relation to anyone living or dead.

Wild Bill Hickok, of course, is real. He was a known gunfighter, gambler, and heavy drinker. In early 1874, he had quit as a performer in Buffalo Bill Cody's Wild West Show. In 1876, he was married in Cheyenne, Wyoming, and then murdered in Deadwood, Montana, while playing poker. Between those times, little is known of his exact whereabouts, but he could well have been on board a gambling boat like the *Astrid Willemina*.

Are Paul and Hannah real? In a way, yes. They are people who have experienced problems, and the choice to overcome them or be ruined by them. They may not be in any Hutterite diaries or history books, but it is my hope that they will come to life in the realm of imagination, giving pleasure, and perhaps drawing the reader a bit closer to God.

Just who are the Hutterites?

In one sense, they are a people locked in time. Named after Jakob Hutter, an early leader, they are the oldest communal-living religious group in the western world. Because the Bible (in Acts 2 and 4) records that early Christians shared their possessions, the Hutterites adopted a communal lifestyle, living together in colonies and co-owning and sharing all of their resources. They continue to live that way today.

Like the Amish and Mennonites, the Hutterites began as Anabaptists. They believed in adult baptism, pacifism, and in living by a direct interpretation of the Bible rather than the rules of the Catholic Church. Because of these beliefs, Jakob Hutter was burned at the stake, and many others were imprisoned, tortured, or executed.

To escape persecution in Germany, Switzerland, and Austria, many Anabaptists sought safety in Moravia, where the Hutterite lifestyle began. They lived there for almost a hundred years before being savagely driven out. Escaping to Hungary, they lived in peace for a time. Then persecution began again, and Hutterite beliefs were almost completely stamped out. They survived only because several wagonloads of Hutterites had been kidnapped earlier and taken to live in Romanian Transylvania, where they were safe for a while. Eventually, more trouble forced them to escape to Wallachia, where the Hutterites once more built colonies—in the middle of an area soon to be fought over by the Turks and Russians. The colonies were repeatedly robbed, and most were eventually burned to the ground by bandits and Turks, who killed many of the men and abused the women.

A Russian general finally saved the Hutterites by giving

them a letter of safe passage to Russia, where they settled peacefully for a hundred years. In 1874, with worrisome changes in the air, Paul Wipf's story begins. The Hutterites are once more ready to move to a new land of promise— America. As the story shows, not all were willing to move at first. Within five years, however, all but a dozen of the original 1,200 Hutterites had left Russia.

What about modern Hutterites?

Hutterites today live according to traditions that are nearly 500 years old. With up to 150 people living in a colony, everyone shares the duties of farming and daily living. They even eat together in a large, communal dining hall. Like the Amish, Hutterites do not believe in using devices like computers, televisions, radios, or musical instruments for entertainment. Unlike the Amish, however, they do use the most up-to-date technology available for their farm work.

The Hutterite lifestyle—from furniture and types of clothing worn, to the age when a couple may marry, to the time when a man must grow a beard—is strictly controlled by the rules of Hutterite tradition. To outsiders, the rule-bound lifestyle may seem restrictive and harsh, yet the people are content, fun loving, and generous. While some Hutterites may have fallen into the trap of living more for colony rules than for God, most have an abiding faith in Jesus Christ that brings contentment and peace.

This faith has given the Hutterites the strength to survive centuries of trouble, to become the prosperous and growing community they are today. There are now more than 40,000 Hutterites, living mainly in the western states and provinces of the United States and Canada.

—*The Author*

Glossary

Hutterite German

Note: Hutterite German, or *Hutterisch*, is not a written language. Hutterites use the High German Bible in church, for scripture reading and sermons, and speak Hutterisch for everyday communication. There is no dictionary of Hutterisch. The invented spellings below represent the sounds of the spoken language.

ach: an exclamation, like "Oh!"

ach, mah Lieba: oh, my love

ansz, zwa, dreia: one, two, three

Ausländischer: outsider or foreigner

Basel: aunt

Butterkuchel: Butterkitchen, a name given to a pig

Checkela: Nickname for Jacob. An endearment, meaning Little Jakey.

Dariusleut: Literally, "Darius people." One of three sects of communal Hutterites, named after Preacher Darius Walter, who was their leader when leaving Russia.

Dei Nomen ist Anfoltich: Your name is Stupid.

du dummer Mensch: you stupid man

Du kennst ihn nit: You don't know him.

Du vorstehts gor nit: You don't understand.

ein Mörder: a murderer

Fater: father

faul Kind: lazy child

Gebet: an evening prayer of thanks

Gemein: the Hutterite community, or colony

Gemeinschaft: a communion, or community of brotherly togetherness and sharing represented by Hutterite colony life

Himble: heaven

Hohna Leber: chicken liver

Ich röd nit Englisch: I don't speak English.

joh: yes (pronounced "yo")

Katus: a cap, or hat

Kinder: children

klana Welt: little world

Lieba: Love, used as a term of endearment

mah: my

Mitz: small cloth cap, worn under the kerchief

Montzleut: Men, or menfolk

Mueter: mother

olten Ankelen: old grandmothers

Pfeffer: pepper

Schmiedeleut: Literally, "blacksmith people." One of the three sects of communal Hutterites. Named after preacher Michael Waldner, a blacksmith, who led the group out of Russia.

Vetter: uncle

High German

Bist du verruckt?: Are you crazy?

Du brauchst eine Frau: You need a wife.

Hammonia: the ship on which the Hutterites crossed the Atlantic

Russian

buran: powerful windstorm

dah: yes

dorak: idiot or fool

Edeetyeh seuda: Come here.

golubka: little pigeon

Isus ljubit tebya: Jesus loves you.

khappers: catchers

kopeck: Russian currency, similar to a penny. There are 100 kopecks in a ruble.

Nye mogu: I cannot.

nyet: no

pappeross: cigarette

Rebyata: children

ruble: The basic unit of Russian currency, worth between $0.43 and $0.50 US in 1874

samogon: a strong, homemade liquor used in Russia

Tsar: King or Emperor

vanka: a slang term meaning "little rascal"

verst: a measure of distance, just under a mile

Notes

Chapter 2—"Didn't the Bible say the disciples shared everything they had with one another so no one would be needy?" Acts 4:32-3.

Chapter 5—Prayers taken from *The Chronicle of the Hutterian Brethren. Vol. 1* (Rifton, NY: Plough Publishing, 1987).

Chapter 8—"*Wie man einen Knaben. . .*" Proverbs 22:6 from the German Luther Bible; "Train a child in the way . . ." Proverbs 22:6 (NIV).

Chapter 10—For information on the death march of the Jewish boy-soldiers, the author is indebted to *My Past and Thoughts: The Memoirs of Alexander Herzen*, trans. Constance Garnett (New York: Alfred A. Knopf, 1973); Gérard Israel's *The Jews in Russia*, trans. Sanford L. Chernoff (New York: St. Martin's Press, 1975); and *Tsar Nicholas I and the Jews: The Transformation of Jewish Society in Russia, 1825-1855*, Michael Stanislawski (Philadelphia: The Jewish Publication Society of America, 1983).

Chapter 34—"You shall not make for yourselves an idol . . ." Exodus 20:4 (NIV).

Most of the information on the Hutterite migration itinerary, including dates, route, and major events on the trip, is taken from these two Hutterite diaries:

1. "Reise Nach Amerika" by Peter Janzen, published in German, in the book *Ansang Von Den Hutterischen Schmieden Gemeinden*, by Hans Decker, Sr. (Hawley, MN: Spring Prairie Printing, 1986). The diary is also excerpted (in German) in the Hutterite history book *Das Klein-Geschichtsbuch der Hutterischen Brüder*.

2. "Diary of the Migration from Hutterdorf to America" by an unidentified Hutterite financial manager from the Darius Walter group; translated into English by Arnold M. Hofer. This diary appeared in *Hutterite Roots*, Hutterite Centennial Steering Committee, Pine Hill Press, 1985.

The Author

Hugh Alan Smith was born and raised in Canada, and lives with his wife, Beth, in Gem, Alberta—a community of about twenty souls.

An award-winning author and teacher, Smith has taught school on a Hutterite colony near Gem for more than twelve years. His classroom is reminiscent of the one-room schoolhouses of yester-year. Traditionally, the communal-living Hutterites permit no computers, videos, tape players, or audiovisual equipment in the classroom. Yet Smith's students have thrived and won awards, including an international geography competition. Ironically, the prizes for this competition included a state-of-the-art computer.

Hugh and Beth are the parents of two daughters: Nicola, married to Kevin Ford, and Danica. Beth is a primary teacher in Gem's small, two-teacher school. The Smiths attend the Victory Church of Brooks, where together they taught Sunday school for nine years.

Hugh Smith holds a journeyman welding certificate and two university degrees in English literature. He has published numerous articles, and co-authored a history resource book and several collections of comedy skits for school and community theater. This is his first novel.